Aliasing

Aliasing

Mara Coson

Semina No. 9

ALIASING

A volcano is about to explode, but perhaps if they don't think about it, it won't happen.

AND THEN THE VIRILE FIRES BEGIN TO RISE UP

VIAGRA-SYRUP LAVA FROM THE LOINS OF
THE WET EARTH'S CRUST

'IT'S HAPPENING, IT'S HAPPENING,'
THE VOLCANO YELLS,

'I'M COMING, I'M COMING, I'M – '

But first –

There was a time that this family was new to Turagsoy.
They say we emerged from the soil one evening, and, if the
rumours are believed, we were formerly catfish. Got the
feeling of having been chosen at random, considering that the
old maid next door climbs up trees in the middle of the night.

Witches, Ma heard, *witches!* She wrenched our front gate
out entirely and built a rotisserie stall with old bricks from
a demolished sugar mill – leaving us with the inconvenience
of having to open the swing door underneath the counter to
get into the house. The door always shut so loud that it could
have been used to make thunder in a radio drama. It is unclear
if, at the time, she knew where the witches were.

We bought chickens cheap from the nearby slaughterhouse,
too small to be sold, and up went the hand-painted styrofoam
'Native Chix' sign. Mama threw them in a pungent chum
and scooped them out from an oil drum, and punched stalks
of lemongrass through the hollowed-out bottoms of the
headless and footless hens, and stuck them in a line on
a forked rod; and they spun from the motor like talc-
powdered baby's chests, with their legs pointed straight
up and their wings held close, as if they were carrying
purses in a crowded boulevard.

Parents taught their kids to look between their legs and
double-check: if from that view Ma disappeared, she was
a witch; if from the same view she was still there, she was
also a witch.

Ma worked as a receptionist at WND Petrochemicals,
and then at Diamond's General Merchandise as a general
all-rounder with some knowledge of metal scanners,
starting pistols, crystal magic balls, male compression

shorts, and condenser microphones. At WND she was commended for her crystal telephone voice, but they put her desk behind a large cement wall with a peephole so that her eyes and mouth had to take turns.

She wore a distinct line of small thin hairs across her face right below both cheekbones, which Mr Diamond surmised was a mark of our past lives as catfish. He also called her a prawn: *Eat the body and throw away the head. Bad luck!* Pilita, my grandmother, had the same problem, though not all the men and women in our extended family, from whom they were estranged, did. *What family and where from?* Shrug.

Our family line started with us, now – from Pilita, the Gaia, to me, the new horizon. It was more peaceful to the mind to leave our origins to the indigenes of Turagsoy. Periodically our grandmother and mother were still sent depilatories and offers to tour the country from circus and teratologists. *But we are no Josephine Boisdechênes, no Clofullias of Vessoix, Switzerland! We do no such thing*, they said. *We are no Mahpoon and Mung Phoset.*

It was snake oil: make the chicken submit, cataleptic, legs up; sweet baste, goodbye to its soul with an unknown prayer behind the great flat rock. (This was the god damn Meteora.) As a matter of personal taste, Ma preferred the dark meat of more sprightly birds for the natural salt that crystallised in their flesh. She trained a grey-eyed dwarf mongrel named Saucisson to catch tikling at the bottom of the mountain, three a day if she was lucky. One she ate, two she sold for a premium. They looked like petrified chickens – not terrified, just medicinal. The Medicinal Native Chix drumsticks stretched out stiff like beckoning fingers and pointed at a ninety-degree angle, but it was a success, even if Ma didn't know which leaf to use for indigestion. These flightless birds had no preservatives at a time when people thought preservatives in food would, in turn, preserve their youth. We were ahead of the curve.

For years, the tikling – wild chickens, barely – rolled there in the rotisserie. They rolled there, and rolled, and rolled and rolled and rolled, one after the other, as the town woke up or slept. For four years, tikling were taken from their chicks as they went out to forage, killed and feathered, hooked up to the electricity, and Ma, waving a stick with a calamus of plastic strips to keep off the flies, stayed open in case anyone wanted a late dinner. The fact that the rods were still turning and always on as the house slept could really make a child nervous.

≈

There was a woman who could always be found in our living room uninvited. Her hair was a perfect marble of white and black, half-and-half, and always greasy; and we just called her 'Belen' because she always took the glazed nativity scene with Jesus in the manger and played with it. For the goat, she vibrated her tongue – *alalala, alelelelele*. We found her inside our lot knocking on the foundations, and she supervised the construction of the arowana pond. Then, there isn't much to say, but she liked to come to the house to comb her hair, a hundred times like they did in the old days, and she said it reminded her, of what, *I can't say*, she said. People claim the house smelled like rotten eggs, especially the gutter. Nobody spoke much when she was there, we just went about things usually done alone, like playing dominos or plucking brows and pits.

One day, Belen announced that she had a new aunt living with her, who was really secretly her mother, and that she could see angels. *What?*

When she said it, I looked up for the first time and I couldn't recognise this person who had been for so long a fishbone in the throat of our lives: the bump on her forehead, the eyes that I have never really looked at, the spacing between them, how boxer-tail her nose was, how a snagged upper canine tooth stretched her left upper lip as she closed it. It was a face I had neither seen nor examined. The whole make-up of the face didn't match my memory of it. Has that happened to you? How could you have never looked properly before? Suddenly it feels like a stranger is in front of you, waiting for a reply to a question which now you must answer. It is a game of pretence, in which you have to respond to show you have always been comfortable with the person.

Once a woman was walking outside my house and she stopped. She didn't move for ten minutes, and it was not required but I had to ask why she wasn't moving. She said that she had forgotten how to walk.

Belen said, *She – can – see – angels*. I didn't want to get into it. I don't believe they exist. But Ma thinks that they are real, because during the visitations of Mother Mary the angels would often arrive on Earth with trumpets and golden sandals.

So, when she came by for lunch and brought over some sweet bread, *No, you really didn't have to*, she said, *Okay, don't eat it though, it's not for you it's to bring to my aunt.*

Let's go then, I said. Her aunt has been living in her house for some time and had completely taken it over, so that Belen felt obliged to ring her own doorbell.

Her house was unfamiliar to me, and anyway I would not see it again. It was the size of a large mausoleum, with columns in front and a large rectangular grey couch that looked like a raised tomb. All the throw pillows were cross-stitched with 'Precious Moments'. Her aunt said, *Welcome and sit, okay*, and the tomb was a comfortable soft lumpen block, and then her aunt said, *So what can this old has-been do for you?* in a disarming professional manner, as if a paid hourly session had begun. She wore very small spectacle frames that looked like kidney beans in front of her eyes, and wore pastel green and pastel pink, with a headband that had spikes so large that it floated above her hair, giving the impression that it was lodged in her skull.

She appears to have been beautiful once, and the large fingerprint mole right in the middle of her nose must have been hairless. She had a strange accent – she stressed every second syllable with a rise and fall, instructive but also worrying, because it felt as though she needed a glass of water or to lie down. By the wall she'd hung photos of herself with celebrities. Strange orbs were in the photographs, some of which were physically scratched out of the prints, to make it appear like they were indeed – *Angels? Yes, yes, angels*, she said.

She stood up close to a frame. Some of the photographs were taken twenty years ago, and she looked like a famous restaurant owner you now barely recognise. *But was that Annie Lennox?*

Your angel is named Gael, and he is three feet tall. He's sitting right there. If you could just kindly put your palm towards the back of your shoulder. There, do you feel that heat? Is he saying anything? *He says you're very special, you're a very special person.* And what else? *He says nothing else. Well, except to tell you that the Mother Mary apparitions are eating into my income, because not only can people see Mother Mary now, like my niece Belen here, but I saw you put the water from our river under her eye with a paintbrush. Don't think I didn't see that, you sly civet. So now people can see showers of petals, diamond leaves and angels acting like the Holy Mother's presidential security guards. You know what that has done to me? Nobody comes to see me anymore, I've had to move out of my apartment in the capital because they wanted to see for themselves. Even the old boil in the Bureau of Customs could see angels, and they say that during the apparitions everybody has their angels standing beside them, and what was I going to do, was I going to say, 'Now I see Mama Mary'.*

≈

Hello?

Hello. We can't hear you right now, oh there. O, yes, ma'am?

I have a question, please.

Go on.

I was shushed by a fellow churchgoer and he accused me of interrupting the Lord's teaching. And I said, *Everybody –*

[Interrupts:] *The historical background of bible scholars tells us that there truly are very outspoken women during*

warship – sorry, worship, that start to non-stop yak while the
teachings are going on. Nenenene, you know, hurts the ears –
yeah, I experience that.

Everywhere the radio was tuned to DWWZ 666. Each
bakery, tarpaulin printer, vulcaniser, resort, condotel, cake
shop, digital media company, bar, cellphone repair shop,
travel agency, shawarma restaurant, chicken rotisserie stall,
pawnshop, cafe, public hot spring, private pool club, gotohan,
nightclub, chapel, Enchanted Kingdom, fast food restaurant,
massage parlour, coconut pie stand, hardware store, grocery
had it constantly on, so that walking through the entire
municipality was seamless.

In ancient times women were not allowed to interrupt those
giving instruction. It says in 1 Corinthians 14:34–35: 'The
women should keep silent in the churches. For they are not
permitted to speak, but should be in submission, as the Law
also says. If there is anything they desire to learn, let them
ask their husbands at home. For it is shameful for a woman
to speak in church.' Isn't it?

I tried to book a ticket for the big city. The travel agency
was brightly painted, periwinkle, and sold whiteners
and 'anti-ageing' creams, including our home-grown iron
water, humic acid, retinoic acid, and a blue spritz serum
that did everything including curing pimples and unclogging
drain pipes. The travel agent, who insisted that for a truly
customised travel experience, I should tell her my life story,
kept winking at everything I said. She asked if I would prefer
to take the cargo ferry or a commercial flight to get there.
I said, *Yes, if you could book me a proper bed suitable for*
my back and she winked again. *So, you would like to see*
the Puñgapung City Zoo?

*And here, also in 1 Timothy 2:11–15: 'Let a woman learn
quietly with all submissiveness. I do not permit a woman
to teach or to exercise authority over a man; rather, she
is to remain quiet. For Adam was formed first, then Eve;
and Adam was not deceived, but the woman was deceived
and became a transgressor. Yet she will be saved through
childbearing – if they continue in faith and love and
holiness, with self-control.'*

I see.

*Do you understand now, girl? 'To be silent' in Greek is
'sigaw'! It means, 'be still'. As in, 'I become silent.' As in
Luke 9:36: 'And when the voice has spoken, Jesus was found
alone. And they kept silent, reported to no one in those days
any of the things they had seen.' But in our language it means
the opposite. It means, 'Shout!' Anyway, Jesus encourages
women to get an education. Thank you for calling.*

Thank you please.

The young teenager in the dried fish stall changed the
station to FM. It's always Michael Learns to Rock. *That's
one reason why I cover you, sleeping child…* There were
boys in basketball jerseys with 'Seattle Supersonics' on
the back, carrying chickens by their legs. *Cover my child,
gonna cover my child…* Three chickens in each hand, and
the chickens viewed the world upside down, gallows humour,
just going with it, as they moved from left to right, stopping
for fun packs.

The chicken had its eyes closed – I thought it was dead
because it looked peaceful, and then it opened its eyes and
closed them again.

There was an upbeat Sunday church service and they were singing worship songs that spoke to the soul, and they sang for ten minutes in the style of Peter, Paul and Mary. They clapped to every downbeat and over-enunciated the 'I' so that it became 'Ha'. *Ha wish that you are who you are, Jesus, ha wish that you are who you are, Jesus, ha wish that you are who you are, Jesus. Ha – right!* Catching the end of the concert was nearly impossible with the padlocks on main staircase and, when the song ended, composure blanketed the entire market and they were able to sell ginger again.

To use the one big lane into the market, at this time, was to be behind the buttocks of two young cows. They seemed agitated in the little trolley that was usually used to transport Shellane or Solane brand gas, and both of them were peeing uncontrollably from their inflamed vulvas, gushing, gushing.

There was a demonstration of a newly formulated seasoning mix at the entrance of the market. They must have hired these demos from out of town, from Puñgapung or some place, because for the proud people of Turagsoy the fish being used was the plague, *even if there was no doubt that the seasoning mix made it delicious.* You never eat snakehead fish. You scoop it out of the water and burn it. You mash it up and turn it into fish bait. Colloquially called 'black mask,' the nickname had no tenderness. It was a cursed fish. A weed. A fish for the aquarium, like the red-bellied piranha, peacock bass, clown knife fish, janitor fish – a monster in its host body of water. DO NOT EAT! *Though it may be delicious…*

Here is a fish, lifted around for everyone to witness its freshness and deadness. *Here is a fish*, she broadcast on her hands-free microphone, an apparatus that looked like a flower that had bloomed from the vine of her hairnet.

Here is a delicious fish. The air-breather was limp in her hands, with its jaw slightly open so that the teeth were on show, though the beast was so dead it couldn't have bitten through a lettuce leaf. The fish was set down on the chopping board, with a portable screen overhead that showed the great predator being scored on the sides so that it would open up when fried, burst open like a red hotdog.

Cindy sold souring agents at the market. Her lover had owned a bar by a sea-diving site until he died in her arms, dancing at a club in the city. That's behind her now, as are the three men she was dating at the same time, including Cowboy, the old mayor. She was in her twenties back then, and had great long oily strands of shimmering hair, like a horse in a moody oil painting in the waiting room of a clinic: three wild horses galloping back from the sea to the shore under a dark and stormy sunset. The horses in these electrifying images are always painted as if they naturally emerged out of the water like mer-equi with new legs, loving life, with a brisk sea wind driving them forward. Cindy's cheeks were still pearly, if not oily, and she was wearing a leaf-print dress. The only patterns she wears are leaves. She once told Ma that she found gumamelas lewd because they looked like open vaginas. *You don't bloom like a flower, you support like a leaf*, she analogised. Cindy found many floral prints too suggestive for a woman in her mid-thirties, and thought it strange how people associated them with meekness. *Ew*.

In this town, she said, people didn't age; people were young, and remained young for sixty-odd years. She also knew that this place had these magical qualities which were in the red water that came out of the taps and went into the cottage soap industry.

Hello Cindy. Sometimes I try to say hello to someone
I'm unsure about greeting by extending my lips sideways
so that my cheeks push forward. This looks like a smile.
Hello Cindy in a wordless gesture, as she bagged citrus
from a sack.

Elena! someone called out, and she turned around.

Over a loudspeaker someone was explaining the miracles
of bottled innard oil. It sounded like a prayer. Beneath
the white speakers, stallholders were playing with their
phones.

I heard the sound of squealing pigs being carried away in
a sack and held pillion on a motorcycle.

There are different types of horses. They're like cars.
You have to test them out. Some of them feel like a Subaru.
Some feel like an owner-type jeep. Oop.

What does this one feel like?

The man climbed onto the horse and ran his cheeks over
its mane.

An owner-type jeep.

You would be lucky if you bought a jeep that gave birth
to a Ferrari.

Behind a fruit and vegetable truck, a cow eyed us as
we caressed the horse's face. It was tied by the nose
so close to the fence that it could only look in our
direction.

Here let me give you a tip. After you test it out for gait,
you check under its eyes to see if it's easily distracted.
Then you check its cowlick – right here – a bad one's
bad luck.

A parked truck with tinted glass was preventing an old
woman and her son getting past. I went up to the vehicle
and knocked on the door. *What the fuck*, the man said,
rolling down his window. He had a huge elbow the size
of a palm heart. *I'm getting out of the parking space, gonna*
back up, they're gonna go through, and then I'm gonna
get out and kill you. So you wait here, you wait here. Since
Cowboy had returned, there'd been a twenty-two per cent
decrease in street violence. A piglet tied to the fence was
crying. *Yes, you sonofabitch*, I said, and as soon as the old
woman and her son inched toward the cow, I ran.

This horse is bad luck.

With my knees pumping, I didn't see the tether a frightened
pug had pulled taut across the path. I tripped, with my right
shoulder landing on mud and small roots. Then I readied
myself for a kick to the head from the startled horse. Never
stand behind a horse on the off chance it might – *Oop*
– down on the ground, belly up like a vulnerable dog. A
cow moved and was trying to say something in a deep low
voice. It positioned its tongue at the roof of its mouth and
sensually slid it down, and time slowed. The sensation was
warm. *What did you say?* But it was just staring. The cow
was still talking. *Listen to these words*, it said. *Listen.* The
children who were watching over the scene said, *Angel*
of God my guardian dear, to whom God's love entrusts
me here, ever this day be at my side, to light and guard
to rule and guide, Amen.

Listen to me. Hnomhnghhhhhh, said the cow. *Hnommmm-mmmmnnggggggggghhhhhhhhhhhth. Do you understand the meaning of the beginning of the song of the journey of this phase of your life?*

The whole world shook. But it was really just shoulders and a man whose company ID said Christopher de Leon, Sales & Marketing. *Hello? Hello? Are you alright? Do you have any broken bones?* Luckily there were none, because the way he shook me, he would have panned any crushed bone down to volcanic ash. Such comfort, having been prayed over, to then be lifted like a child or a toy poodle with my buttocks in his hands. My blood fell on the hand towel he had placed to catch the sweat on his back.

A friend told me that when she was learning to ride, a kid got kicked by a horse. He just lay on the ground with his eyes open. Before this incident he was a dumb ox, and afterwards he had a dent in his skull and became a software engineer.

And then I spied my angel-seeing aunt approaching me. She had a coin slot's underbite and was singing '25 Minutes'. *Christopher de Leon, thank you but please go on your own way, and thank you again! Excuse me, angel-seeing aunt. Did Gael angel tell you anything about a cow?*

She was so happy to be recognised, in the way someone who doesn't recognise you is happy to see you, just because you might be someone they need to keep onside. She started to mouth the entire question again, but then began to look upset.

What did the angel say about the cow?, I asked.

How dare you, nobody likes to be tested, do you know that?

*Nobody is testing you, there's no choice left but to believe
in Jael, Gael, Michael, and Rafael, and all the angels and the
saints who have done God's will throughout the ages – but
tell me if you can see these angels, tell me what the cow said!*

≈

*You know we don't like strange people. Strange rhymes
with change. We don't like those circus freaks that come
to our town and sing songs. I mean what is that? They can't
even sing. We don't like people saying there are monsters here,
what? In my town there are no monsters, shit, we don't have
things that fly. We have, what? We have dragon flies, we have
fireflies, we have butterflies. We have head lice, house flies,
fruit flies, vinegar flies. I'll tell you a story about a movie
I watched when I was a boy, a movie named* Fury. *You
know Dick Tracy – he was a detective? And Sylvia Sidney?
The old witch Pilita who lives on Penis Hill is a big fan.
She's a nobody! I saw her again in* Mars Attacks *when the
aliens came to her room and heard the song 'I'm Calling
Youuuu…' and their heads exploded. See, that's what happens
to strange people: I'm calling youuuuuhuu… Explode. Fritz
Lang, son of a bitch, directed* An American Guerrilla in the
Philippines *in 1950 – right here in Turagsoy – because he liked
the volcano that's about to – and then when my grandfather,
the former mayor, said 'Come to my house for dinner', Lang
stiffed him, son of a bitch. So, in the movie, you know, this
innocent guy was about to marry his fiancée, he was just
saving up and then driving to meet her. Decent man. And
you know, he loved eating salted peanuts. I love peanuts too.
In a town he drove through, three women were kidnapped.
So, the cops stopped him and he had a wad of cash because*

*he was going to his fiancée's, and so he was interviewed by
a detective at the police station, who said,* Would you like
some peanuts? *The innocent guy said,* I love peanuts, I never
leave without them. *A-ha! The kidnapper also liked peanuts.
He must be the kidnapper. Oh well, let's not rush to a
conclusion. The reporter who was there looking for a beat
said,* Oh! So they found the suspect! *But the detective is a
limp dick, a limp Dick Tracy. So, he said, 'I will go off and
tell my friends, and I think we should take this matter to our
own hands. Yeah! Round up a bunch of people, yeah!' said
the reporter. A big mob goes to the jail, you know, and they
beat up the detective and ransack everything; mayhem, you
know, and they burn the man in jail. And his fiancée comes
but can't save him and just watches as he burns. OK? That's
what happens to strange people. We don't give them the time
– when we know, the public knows, the evil they commit.
You know. My father brought peace and order to this
community. Your ancestors were evil men, always killing each
other. Ah shit, my great-grandmother was a small-time crook,
so you know what my grandfather did? He killed her! He
removed all those strange people in your family too – I will
not say any more. You know who they are, those com… and
those hom… We like everything natural. Punks! I know there
are still many strange people, and we will destroy them! They
have infiltrated our church, our market. They have infiltrated
our pet shops. They bring in Fong Shit. You know, the things
that God creates, like, what's that, the one that – ? We don't
like strange people. And this thing, I mean, this talk, about
mythological creatures – stop that. Stop that. Stop those folk
tales about what you see at night. I'm tired of hearing that we
have these things that dismember, phantoms that dismember
people. The only people we dismember are the ones who talk
about this shit. So, remember, if you want to continue to be
a member of my community, be a law-abiding citizen of this*

great town of Turagsoy, don't be strange. Don't cross me,
don't tell me lies, don't sing, don't threaten to put me in
jail, don't hallucinate, don't say the volcano is about to –
don't cause trouble. Don't cause trouble. Let me be clear:
I AM COMING.

≈

They say the monster has fourteen bones in its neck and can
turn its head to see from behind. Through its large yellow eyes,
it sees perfectly at night. It whinnies like a horse. *I believe*
there is a mare on top of the tree, sir. It sits at the top of the tree
and appears at times to have morphed with the branches. The
tree is a strangler so be careful, sir. In the dense forest it latches
onto a host tree, grows around it, setting down its roots and
completely possessing it. Be careful, sir. They say there is
half-goat, half-human creature, and it's come to kill, sir.

You mean near where we…? Cowboy whispered to his aide,
and wiped his pointing finger across his neck. *Yes, Sir, near*
where we…

Okay, okay, you cowards, he'd announced, *I'll investigate that*
son of a bitch, let's get it! We went into the forest, whose main
path was only two right turns from the city hall. *Anyone going*
to the toilet before we go – particularly the women in the search
crew? Okay, no women here, except my son Bayot. Ha! Okay
let's go.

Cowboy often embarked on these missions, with or without
a film crew. *I'm just doing my job, ma'am,* he'd say to the
camera. He preferred not to be filmed, he'd tired of acting.
Shooting meant that he could not actually shoot, and anyway,
it comes with a director and he despised directors. He hated

how the rest of his kumpadres would put their arms around a director and ask for acting tips. *What do directors know? They're not actors! They're not even lackeys! They're shit!*

They reached the tree, and from up high something whinnied. It was so loud that Cowboy ducked, and then, upon regaining his composure, he knocked out his son Bayot with the butt of a pistol. *You're a coward!* He yelled, *You are all cowards.* Then Cowboy asked one of his masked men to climb it. He had barely climbed two feet when he complained, *Sir, with these masks it's very hard to climb in the evening, I can barely see.*

Idiot! Who told you to cover your eyes with it? He took a rock and threw it at the man's head. He climbed up himself. He used to do this often as a child. It's different at night, and water was spilling out from the big grandfather-roots. Cowboy was expecting a duel. Would bullets pierce the beast? Would he have to knock him fistfuls between the eyes? He got to the top of the tree and located the source of the frightful whinnying. It was an owl.

Sabotage!, he howled. He twisted the screech owl's neck, but because of its fourteen bones and ability to turn 270 degrees, Cowboy had to twist the owl's head, and twist the head and twist the head again. Cowboy shot the owl, and it whinnied until it landed in a small stream that carried it away. The search crew were laughing.

Who set me up?

We didn't set you up, sir. Cowboy shot the entire search crew dead. Bayot woke up with the sun and saw that the creature had killed everyone.

≈

If you walk the town's littoral zone at low tide, bleached corals replace the sand and the beach looks like it has eczema. There are congregations of sea shells near big rocks, like a parking lot, a community hall, a gambling den, the boulevard on a Friday night. They're the parked cars of hermit crabs, and the tunnels they've dug into the sand could be mistaken for human ears. Inside the bigger holes there are sea urchins hiding with their spikes drawn around them, like a fence of dry grass. If it wasn't for the sound of Survivor's 'Ever Since the World Began' from a nearby team-building karaoke gathering, you could hear them gurgling: Shells adjusting inside their houses, cleaning out last night's excrement, waiting for darling.

We have waited for this mo-ment to di-e... ever since the world began...

There was a bar near the water owned by a couple in their fifties with a hairless terrier. They were crouched down, cracking open sea urchins they had gathered in a plastic bag and bottling them. The marlin they caught from the sea was as large as a mermaid's bottom half, and they hung it upright so that it looked like the creature was half submerged in sand.

I used to call my dogs 'Stephanie' and 'Jennifer', until a neighbour asked me, *Why had my dogs been given human names, and why so very American?*

The bar was set between the shore and the water and was made of bamboo tied with twine and nylon. It bore a neon sign of a mermaid lying down on the beach, but nobody had ever seen it on. It just hung like a light-reflected ghost. Most

of the barflies came in the afternoon anyway. The bar
wrapped around a sick mango tree whose warty fruit hit
drunks as they stumbled home.

One night, Girly told all of us that she and her British
husband Mark were aliens from outer space. One hand
on the Blow Job cocktail she was making, the other to
her chest, she said she was relieved to make this confession
that, ever since, she has compulsively repeated.

To whoever asked, they were Anbau (husband and former
chemist from Shropshire, now bar owner) and Shla (wife
and biologist, now bar owner). They said that they had
not expected to crash here and needed a full set of repair
instructions, which was taking a long time to arrive, to
get their ship back up and running.

They always wore robes with vertical stripes of silk, and
backs that had a dragon on them, as if they were two separate
robes sewn into one, perhaps the result of indecision.

The bar's patrons weren't surprised by the revelation and
started to wonder if maybe they too were aliens…

No, but I really am one;

Yeah, well I never knew my parents.

*When I nap I experience sleep paralysis and talk to silver-
skinned beings in campaign T-shirts about the Senate.*

*I have been in three car crashes in which everybody died,
including the aunt of the late dictator, and I escaped without
a scratch.*

I seem to experience life in two second intervals, like a pigeon's head, only slower.

I have an enormous sexual appetite at sunset.

I move my forearm up and down over a sick person's body, like a scanner, and my arm hairs burn where it hurts.

My mother always wanted me to be like the author of that Winged Pharaoh *book...*

What?

We always got copies of her books at the American surplus shop my family ran. They called the book, Far Distance, *was it?* Far Memory? *I can't remember now.*

Two more Weng Wengs, please, Girly.

My mother said that if I wanted to be a true citizen of the world but didn't have the money to travel, I needed to read. That's where you get the true essence of life. I think that's true, and she liked to think that she was well-read. When her journalist friends came to drink beer, she hid her Ludlums in the bathroom. But I knew I carried a lot of demons in my life, a lot of pain, in my childhood – in my mind, I can't even enter the room where my father ate.

Go on.

No, don't go on, Girly pleaded.

My mother said the Winged Pharaoh *was written in a trance, with the author reciting her life as Princess Sekeeta. I believed her because she could see ghosts, and, you know, her mother was a psychic. You know, she could recall her past lives too.*

You're bringing a lot of negative energy in here, no? Mark said, opening the window and swatting the bad air out with repeated flicks of his wrist. *I have to rearrange the furniture now. God, if lifting this bar didn't scatter the cockroaches. Oh, look – you're scaring Girly.*

And her mother predicted the Titanic.

Mark lifted up the knife he was cutting limes with:
This is your, The End, Joe! This is your, The End!

From then on, they always talked about their alien lives. Sometimes their whole home was made of steaming hot moss, and sometimes all matter was comprised of lichens with brains, and sometimes it was made of zirconium. Soon after, they lost the bar and the dog because they were swindled into debt by a sleeping business partner. Then they lost the entire dive site, which they had to sell to a resort developer, and then it became the scene of a future massacre.

They stopped their conversation to listen to a bird call. *It's that one*, said Girly. *It's a bad omen for us, all this violence and skewering.* That bird impales its prey on thorny bushes, collecting impaled frogs, lizards, and amphibians to attract mates.

Why do you think we ended up in this shithole?, Mark asked. Their spaceship was two kilometres away in the water, and they would always look out to it as if it was the key to their entire life, and they needed to stand guard by the sea. Their house was round like an igloo and it was algae green, with

a Jacuzzi inside, right in the middle. It was strange that
the entire lot was always colder than everywhere else on
the island.

John Rand, a scientist, had explored Turagsoy in 1964 and
noticed, in his daily walks around the uninhabited portions
of land, congregations of dead snails in the undergrowth,
whose meat had been removed from the broken shells. Rand
ruled out monkeys, and he discounted human agency because
the snails were at a difficult angle to reach, and therefore not
worth such effort for this lazy genus.

The power went off at the bar and killed the electric dart
board. Whenever this happened, we all said, *Fuck the King!*
But we had no king. At dusk the patrons looked out on
the sea and took in the sick dead fish floating on the water,
catching the light of the setting sun and sending it back out.
Kingfishers dived into the water to catch the carrion.

A woman entered the pitch-black bar. Her hair was a
mess, covering her whole face, and there was a small slice
of seaweed attached to the top of her head. Her shirt was
torn, or maybe it was already distressed when she bought it.

Jesus Christ!, said Mark. *A mermaid!*

Water, said the woman.

Fuck the King!

The lights went back on.

Belen! She was bleeding from her forehead and had cuts on
her arms and knees. *My aunt, I mean, my mother, wasn't who*

she said she was... Was she my mother? Where is my wallet? Where am I?

Belen! Ma cried, *Belen, here I am!* ¡Sacar estar!

Rand deduced the killer was a bird. But which species? One day he dissected a kingfisher, laying its red orange plume and violet chest and long brick-coloured beak out on a metal tray, and there was snail meat in its intestines. The bird would choose the perfect rock, take the snail in its bill, lift its head up and smash the shell hard against it.

Rand also noted that the lammergeier, a bearded vulture, ate tortoises by carrying them high into the sky and dropping them against a carefully selected rock to break open their shells in order to get at the meat.

Pilita looked at Belen from the edge of the bar and extinguished her cigarette on the clasp of her twenty-four carat Bolex. *Over my dead body is that woman staying with us.*

Pliny recounted that a lammergeier had lifted a tortoise very high up and then dropped it on the bald head of Aeschylus, the Father of Greek tragedy.

≈

In the kitchen, where Zonrox bleach evaporated sweetness from the tiles, Belen, with her lampshade pleat duster, kept her ear by the Sanyo radio to listen to primetime drama: kissy kissy, moaning, foley sex, while outside in the heat, calicos flipped a mouse until the rodent disappeared somewhere behind the louvered cabinet and died there.

Pilita says that around the late nineteen-thirties, Hollywood used to send pre-code talkies to the colonies, dirt for dirt, particularly the films that failed with American audiences. She used to sneak out and watch films like *Merrily We Go to Hell* by Dorothy Arzner at the town theatre; but it came to Turagsoy without sound. Pilita had to guess what Jerry Corbett said to Joan Prentice (Sylvia Sidney). It changed my grandmother's life. She learned to clap whenever the mechanical leather bags prompted the audiences to applaud until they learned to do so on their own.

But let's fast forward to the news that a conwoman named Helena Pedroche had claimed she was the illegitimate daughter of former President Marcos, a major shareholder of the Mandarin Oriental, a pilot for Virgin Atlantic, an employee of the UK Home Office, and a Campbell's soup heiress. With her royal treatment from the Mandarin Hotel, she had charmed several unsuspecting people and become their best and most generous friend, so it was only fair for them to help her in return, loan her money beyond their means when she needed money to access her rightful Marcos billions, out of which the principal and much more would be returned. Today, she owes hundreds of thousands of pounds to overseas nurses, lobster sellers, and a Swedish woman.

I tell you, Pilita said within earshot of Belen, *We call her Belen, Belen-Belen, but we don't even know her real name – for all we know it's HELENA PEH-DRO-CHEH.*

≈

Mice dulled their long teeth and chewed through the electrical wiring, causing our school to explode into flames, the grade-repeater accused of arson explained as we watched the fire come out of the doors. Mice carry parasites that make them desire cat urine. Holding onto his cool, he tried to make sounds with the rim of a glass beaker. *It wasn't me*, he said. These mice *sneak a little lick of piss*, he said, *and then are swiftly eaten by the cats* – the ultimate goal of the parasite being to infect felines. He smashed the beaker. We took him to the hospital.

An old piano-playing bartender companion – who once said that the secret of beer is you never sip it, you gulp it because it tastes terrible, and nobody drinks beer for the taste – had heard on the radio that cat ladies *become* cat ladies by inhaling cat poo. They breathe in a parasite and the strain lodges itself in the human brain, telling these incumbent cat ladies that they must take care of the pitiful animals.

The grade-repeater would one day become a colonel, and one night the bartender was tickling the ivories at the local boozer, and the drunken colonel said, *Shut the fuck up!* and then shot her dead.

The news stinger interrupted an adaptation, for Catholic Radio, of sexual relations between real-life estranged lovers using the names Jun and Dovie, to announce the campaign-trail comeback and subsequent admission into the Intensive Care Unit of a government official running for President, who had explained that a new anti-cancer medicine would bring back her personality, whereas the current prescription made her weak. She said that the new drugs were very expensive, and her sister, a doctor in America, was helping her, and that being largely absent from the campaign trail was not a problem. She narrowly missed election twenty years ago, but, currently polling only three per cent of the vote so far, would widely miss it this time. The campaign favourite announced that he would fatten up the fish in the ocean with the corpses of 100,000 dead drug pushers. This is an immortal line.

Pilita said that during the war people ate cats because there were lots of them and not much of anything else, other than rats if the cats didn't get to them first. Cat meat has the texture of kapok. They also tried to eat swamp spinach but died of bloated ankles and were found floating in rivers as if they had been on inflatables in a swimming pool. Ma told her that it is difficult to tell the difference between a skinned rabbit and a skinned cat. *Have you ever seen a rabbit? Yes of course, they are grey and walk on two legs.*

She never ate anything that appeared to be the size of a cat. Unless it was a chicken. The newsflash stinger came back on to say that the sick candidate had passed away. Pilita said a prayer.

≈

As a child, I used to visit the bar of Mark and Girly in the afternoons to watch all of these American television shows. Not that we couldn't afford our own set, but my mother was afraid that televisions would accelerate the world into *The End*. Eventually we did get cable.

Mark was particularly taken with Charlton Heston. Sometimes Pilita joined us: *Now that's my kind of man!* Charlton Heston in his standout role as Moses in *The Ten Commandments*. Charlton Heston in *Planet of the Apes*, *The Omega Man*, *The Agony and the Ecstasy*, *The Naked Jungle*, *Touch of Evil*, *Three Violent People*, *Two-Minute Warning*, *The War Lord*, and Charles Heston in a videotaped

episode of *What's My Line*. Mark bore a resemblance
to Charlton Heston, an actor I, for a very long time,
called 'Charlie Stone', because of the way Pilita said it.

I love the 1956 episode of *What's My Line* that Mark
and Girly played over and over again at the bar. The show
was hosted by John Daly and featured Charlton Heston as
celebrity guest, with Arlene Francis, Douglas Fairbanks Jr.,
Dorothy Kilgallen (a journalist whose investigation into the
assassination of JFK may have been a cause of her mysterious
'drug overdose' in 1965, on a bed that she may not have often
regularly slept on), and Random House publisher Bennett
Cerf (who married the actress Sylvia Sidney) on the panel.

Cerf, in his usual manner, introduced host John Daly: *I think
you may be interested to know that when General Moose
Stillman, the commandant of the US Air Force Academy, met
him in Denver recently, he was poorly briefed and thought
that John Daly was Carroll John Daly the mystery story
writer. So, he spent the entire lunch talking about mystery
stories and couldn't understand why he didn't get much
response. So here he is, John Charles Sherlock Holmes Daly.*

Carroll John Daly pioneered the first 'hard-boiled private
eye' fiction in the early twenties but his celibate hero lost
the readership. When asked about Mickey Spillane, who
had based his character Mike Hammer on Daly's Race
Williams but made his dick much racier and hyper-sexual,
Daly could only say, *I'm broke and this guy gets rich
writing about my detective.*

In this episode: a woman named Jean Chapman, a ferry
boat pilot from Vallejo, California – *Do you wear a costume
other than an ordinary sort of dress when you're performing*

this service?, Milton Meier, a worm raiser from Priddy, Texas – *I beg your pardon, 'Priddy, Texas'? Yes, it is, actually, I must say – and how are you, Dr Dubious? Oh no, that's wrong, wrong line*, and Bob Foss who owned and operated a Turkish Bath – *Am I right in assuming that, that that that, it wouldn't matter if a man were married or a bachelor, he would still be – am I right in assuming that you need not be alone in performing your services – it can be done, you don't mind if...* I didn't know at the time what a Turkish bath was, and because Mark knew that I would ask, he immediately said I couldn't ask. This was one of the few times we actually spoke. He was a person with a completely different life to the one I knew, so confidently otherworldly it frightened me.

They put on wonderful silk eye masks, and then Charlton Heston walked in.

May I assume that you're not Ale-vis?

I beg your pardon, Dorothy?

May I assume you're not Elvis?

Mark watched a lot of Douglas Fairbanks, and when the waters were rough he played *The Mystery of the Leaping Fish*, where Fairbanks played a cokehead parody of Sherlock Holmes. Pilita said it was the first Hollywood film to have played in Turagsoy.

Speaking of leaping fish – well, it didn't leap but showed its side... There was once a young family that came to Turagsoy on a staycation to get a break from their father who was paralysed by a stroke. They belonged to a group of people that claimed to have seen a mermaid in the resort. And then they got a call from their father. *Pa?!*

He called up and said that he was thirsty and asked for water and some food, and said, *Well, it's fun to swim in the water.*

A miracle!

The resort manager observed, *It's been such a great opportunity for us since that mermaid went viral.*

They then collected the water from around the sighting, an impossible task, and considered it blessed.

When the news staff checked with the resort staff they said, *No, it isn't a mermaid, we have a video of it – here – that creature has come up close to us on several occasions. That is a dugong: a sea cow.*

Ay! Pilita screams! *Ay!*

Are you dying, Pilita? Is it your time?

She swats her arm around as if she was dancing to the tune of *Let the Joy Rise.*

Something is flapping around in the bar, sending the whole place into a panic!

Mark turns on the light.

A bird is trapped inside the bar! Cover the mirrors! Fuck the King!

≈

It is said that myths and legends are used to scare people
out of doing things when a regular reprimand will not do.
*There are witches that make magic with real estate tax and
Tamaraws disappear – the Toyota kind.*

Could it be that people who engage in these practices quietly
come together and agree on a particular legend, over fighter's
liquor? *We will claim that we saw this creature here, and that
it comes from behind the tree on the night before a half moon,
and that it runs? No, that it walks very slowly, and then it
runs. That way, we can keep this mansion away from the rest
of the inheritance-grabbing distant cousins.* Maybe there are
hundreds of such pacts.

Once, Ma found a photo of us in an American newspaper
that had been taken when we were washing our pants in
the mangrove:

A serene morning view of local witches.

≈

Call me Jerry, said the fat Shih Tzu breeder friend of Ma's
whose weakness was gin. *Oh shit*, he took it back. *Call me
Wicky.* He had a short tongue. He was introduced to her
friends Maggie, Lilibeth, and Letty.

Girls, this is…

Hi, I'm Wicky. Hi Wiwibeth. Wetty. Waggie.

But he just said his name was Jerry.

I breed Shih Tzus.

Hi, Wicky.

While Ma was in the bathroom I came in and told her,
I hate Jerry.

Close the door, the smell!

Ma always said, *Hate is too strong a word*. It was, to her,
worse than *shit*. She spat out her toothpaste with some gum
blood. To dislike his cigar – his cigar became Jerry. To dislike
his membership of the local PO3 Harley Davidson club
– none of the motorcycles were actually Harleys, they were
all Jerry. The big round shell-back couch he sat on became
Jerry, the way he put his tongue out when he smoked a cigar
as if to catch it became Jerry, the way his hands stretched out
and his knuckles sank into dimples became Jerry, the way he
exposed his buttocks when he bent over to pat the dachshund
became Jerry, the dachshund became Jerry, the stench he left
of mildew and saliva became Jerry, until nearly everything
from that one encounter became Jerry.

Jerry wore large gold-plated bracelets on both wrists, and
when he laughed he slapped his thigh and lifted his feet up,
and each time he did it he laughed a *heaux heaux*, more than
a ha ha, which was disconcerting, and his teeth were fully
zirconium. Jerry was particularly skilled at telling people how
good he was at killing mosquitoes. He never missed. His clap
created a vortex where the force of two fat hands forcing the
wind through a central point trapped a mosquito, arrested its
wings, and readied it for the kill. The mosquito fell on white
Formica. I looked in closer and saw its legs spread open as
a last gesture before death.

I hated his hair. It stuck out like a gelled pubis, forced down to cover the top of the head as though carefully secured with Saran Wrap. I felt that I could no longer trust Ma for lying with him. I know because we all slept in the same room with Pilita, not because the chicken business hadn't blessed us with enough money to leave the town and re-emerge elsewhere as fish, but because we had forgotten to get out and it was too late and pitch black and they were having a moment of passion. The whole time their bodies jigged around the room I was overcome by the stench of rancid meatballs.

Jerry wanted to be everybody's best friend, trying to make light of everything except his dreams, giving advice that people didn't realise they'd never asked for. The most frequent thing Jerry said was, *Time is of the essence.* It became possible to believe that he had been first to say it, that he owned it. I hate the word 'essence', I hate the sound of it! Processing the life out of leaves and seeds, squeezing out their extractable juices, spinning them on a centrifuge, and then bottling them for fake dermatologists in commercials, who would nod in the background while a woman with a Velcro towel around her head splashes her face with water before applying the cream. Essence. And how is time of the essence? Of which particular plant's essence? I collapsed onto the carpet because I was tired of hearing it, and I wanted to pull each hair out of the carpet and I tried. I saw, out of the corner of my eye, a large rat, and then I went back to trying.

Jerry also began to spend a lot of time at the gambling house which faced a large cluster of pet supply stores owned by Feng Shui Master Yeung Bi Bi. Jerry went there quite regularly, and one promising day he brought home an arowana in a large tank. Yeung Bi Bi was only the shop owner's Feng Shui name, for this was a sideline of our Mayor Cowboy's. In order to control the strange and ludicrous exploitation of the town's spoils he had to become its endpoint. He already ran the port and the gambling houses. Jerry regretted that the green-back arowana was a tame choice, and that if the family hadn't pestered him so much he would have brought home an alligator like a real man, because his friend Fr. Low had an alligator living in his swimming pool; but our house didn't even have an outdoor faucet. *If you wanted to know what kind of smuggled goods were in there*, he said, *well...* Jerry winked and laughed, lifting his feet up and slapping his thigh.

Jerry had to collect crickets inside a twelve-litre bucket for the arowana, also called Jerry, and I thought the crickets would jump out but he said they couldn't jump that high. *Quiet! Shut up you!* I yelled, with both forefinger and thumb pointed like a gun at the house's money area, in the practice of Feng Shui. *They can't hear you*, he yelled, *they have made themselves deaf.* Each night the crickets wailed outside the bedroom door, which, adding to the guilt over the chickens, the sound of the rotisserie rods slowly spinning, made it impossible to sleep until I got so used to all of them that I couldn't sleep without them.

In 1950, Fritz Lang came to the capital en route to Turagsoy to shoot a war film that he later considered to be the worst movie he ever made. He came to the radio station KZRM because he was listening to the radio while on set and he was amazed at the sound bites they got, from everyone from Chiang Kai Shek to Joseph Stalin. He went to KZRM and found out that a man named Koko Trinidad had been impersonating them: *The easiest way to control the population is to carry out acts of terror!*

*Yesterday in the news there was a Swiss man who was killed
not far from here. His name was Roger Fritz Lang. He was
playing basketball in a village, or a cluster of houses, and he
got into a fight and was stabbed with a knife. No, he came
out of his house to tell the boys playing outside to be quiet.
He was sixty-seven. A Samaritan intervened as he scolded
the boys, but the kids stabbed him and ran.*

So, you say he was hung, and chop-chopped, the man on the
radio told the perpetrator. *But in your affidavit here, on page
thirty-five, you said his throat was slit and he was stabbed
all over. I just want to get the facts straight.*

No, we hung him, a group of us, and he was chop-chopped.

All aspirational families have more arowanas than dogs
because everyone here read a circular claiming that the
fish bring good luck according to Feng Shui Master Yeung
Bi Bi. The arowana is also known as the bonytongue,
not because it appears to move in the water as if it was
a long tongue with bones, which might have been the
case – like Jelly Tongue, which was a neon green frozen
jelly in the shape of a tongue that our school banned
us from eating because the principal believed it was like
French kissing – but because of a bone at the bottom tip
of its mouth that appears to look like its actual tongue,
but with teeth. The arowanas bring good luck because
their shiny scaled bodies and whiskers make them look
like dragons, and so they are in every rich man's home;
or every rich man who can afford them, or every poor man
who spends his money on an arowana and hopes to get his
money back and as a consequence finds himself forced to
earn a small fortune to pay off the debt incurred. Arowanas
understand the words we speak and can foretell the future.

They also fill their owners' homes with positive energy and absorb negative energy.

Belen, being the newest in the family, always had to replace the arowana's water. *Arowana, arowana, arowana do this*, which then became simply *arowana*, and she used the word for many other things she didn't wanna do. And then, *It's Diego Salvador! On the radio!*

There will come over the Earth a great darkness,
the air stagnant, lacking oxygen. There will be no light;
the candles will be few. Then the heat will become intense.
– Mother Mary, through Veronica Lueken, 1973

The timing of your arrival has been particularly uncertain.
All prognostication is bleak, whether pamphlet low or satellite
high: the volcano is going to…

≈

It is not something to watch. It is not conjoined vases.
It is not a Fushigi ball. It is not a boil with pus. It is not
breast milk spilling from the nipple. It is not the sex tape
of a Senator or the Late Dictator of the New Society.
We are in the permanent danger zone.

We live in Turagsoy, a second-class municipality that
lays like gum stretched between an ocean and a lake that
contains a volcano along the Pacific ring of fire. Largely
unknown to the rest of the country because it is neither
city nor province, Turagsoy is a cartographical oversight;
chicanery; the black hole on the tip of the tongue; the
illusion of *x* and *o* on far sides of a paper with one
eye closed.

My house stands by a tall lava-rock build-up from a previous eruption. *'Do not build'* was displayed on the same pole as our street sign. We wash clothes along a thin string of iron-rich river washed out like blood from a chicken sliced at the neck under a sink, running down the drain and into the ocean. Many in Turagsoy earn money from its whitening potential. *Later in this tour, you will be able to purchase soap and also water bottled at the source.*

Welcome and careful of the half-step.

I volunteered at the tourist centre at the foot of Mt. Tabor, a raised hut made of marine plywood with light green curtains.

Several hundred years ago Tabor erupted and the explosion sliced off the top of the volcano to reveal a crater lake, and then created a smaller growth beside it. It is to this new outcrop that we mistakenly ascribe the image of volcano – of the Tabor in particular – especially as viewed from the resorts of Bunganga. So many photographs and postcards! But it is not the volcano. It is not where the crater lake is.

I looked at it through the satellite photos of the local government's Dell computer. *Don't touch the mouse with your fingers. Zoom in.* How did we never notice that it was in fact the mountain behind it?

Aaaaaaaaaaaaaaaaaaaaaaaaaaaaaaaaaaaaaaaaaaaaaaaaaaaaaaaaa aaaaaaa

Aaaaaaaaaaaaa

In the middle of the small lake, a finger poked through a tiny hole.

When we printed the crater lake on shirts and ordered
China-made snow globes that go black when shaken and
embossed the image on toadskin coin purses, we were
sued by the town of Bunganga.

It's not your volcano, ours has the real crater lake, we said.
*Yours glistens like a ceramic tagine, a phallic elongation
on a pottery wheel, public art, ha ha*, we explained, and
anyway it was dormant because it was not even a volcano,
it was only a view.

But it is.

And that is a small sample of the region's politics. Moving
forward, our caldera – the inner lake, a lake on an island
on a lake on an island, the lake-within-a-lake – a doughnut
volcano with the explosions that once caused the entire
capital centuries ago to have candlelit lunches with the
smell of rotting eggs for months afterward, and people
*walked about the streets confounded and thunderstruck,
clamouring for confession during the eight days that the
calamity was visible.*

The mountain is filled entirely with the corpse flower, red
and spotted exactly like the firefly gecko found only on the
same peak. Taking sustenance from the big unruly tabatib
vines, the parasite rafflesias, stuck out in bloom, are the
mountain's metre-wide assholes, a strange growth that, on
show, releases a badness inside and gives the town a smell
of dead rats.

The firefly geckos, or tuko, grew to the size of wild cats.
An old chronicler, Fray San Antonio, says of them: *The
salamanders (who, some say, are the lizard of Chapter 30*

of Proverbs, No. 28) have claws so sharp they can cling to a mirror. These on our mountain are gold and red and glowing. You could sell them for the price of a house and lot, if you could catch one without touching it.

Our volcano also had a whole forest of high kapok. The trees are being eaten by the termites so it appears that they have veins like humans, varicose tracts across their arms. These are majestic trees from the Americas that yield a wild and unruly cotton, only used for stuffing. The pillow I slept on was made of the kapok tree. Each kapok pod would burst open into a white puff much like Bichon Frise dotted with many, many eyes, and the white curly cotton dogs would fly everywhere. *Snow! Snow! It's not snow children, get inside, you'll get asthma. Please turn on the nebuliser and lock the house. Pray for your own safety.* But the kapok tree sap can prevent asthma. The kapok tree is unguarded, it is wild, and when a man once tried to chop down its hoof-like roots, his body was found on the church steps with its legs severed.

After lunch on a day as hot as breath, I assisted a small tour group comprising two local families, my mother, a Dominican priest and a German geologist. My tour group rode up on horseback through the trail of sinking volcanic ash, up and down and curved right and swerved left. I found it difficult to walk up in slippers because the stubble of ash stuck to my soft feet. So, I too rode a horse.

It was hard to get on the horse, and it took me several tries to get my leg up over the thigh. The veins on my leg pinched, and after successfully getting on and thrusting my pelvis too close to the neck of the horse I kept sliding off. I was worried if I sat on the lowest point of its spine and if I stayed on I would injure its back permanently.

The group followed me. It was inevitable that they would get tired, especially climbing up and down the unfinished parts of the trail where it got particularly soft and sandy but in a colour that you couldn't distinguish from manure.

As we got up the hill, I told everyone, *dive forward*. What? I meant, *lunge forward*.

Thank you for emerging today, Ale told those who had come up the hill.

What?

Thanks for coming up the mountain today.

I stood atop a boulder and said, *Welcome to the crater lake. And careful of the half-step*. It was difficult to imagine that we had made it to the top, and it looked like the earth had piled up to block our view. There was a bald spot in the vegetation left from when the volcano had last exhaled smoke. The water was warm. *The water*, I said, *is so sulphuric that nothing can live in it – not even mosquitoes.*

The pez mulier! cried the man beside me on the tour. He was a holidaying geologist whose hairy legs had burn marks from an overly vigorous Swedish massage in a local parlour.

What, Sir? For emphasis, I prefer to put the 'H' before the 'W', so that it sounds more commanding.

The pez mulier! I have never seen one in my life and never expected to see one in freshwater. He was pointing to creatures that were pink and naked, oiled, with human-like sex organs. *Why have you caged them!*

HWAT SIR.

He pointed again. They looked like humans, with alert eyes.
Look at their heads, look at them look at us! Them look at us!
I'm crying. Fresh water. Their heads, they're like baseball caps,
or penis heads, and the male one has a penis, and the woman
is suckling her young with her breasts. Look at her breasts!
Look at them swim together.

I don't see them Sir. You mean they are mermaids?

No. They are absolutely not. He assembled his gun, aimed at
a lone pez mulier and shot twice, missing only once. I flinched
and nearly slid into the water where a young family of pez
muliers were swimming until they dispersed in a frenzy and
blood began to colour the water. The pez mulier cried like
a child as it died, *I thought so*, he said. *Come help me get this.*

No! I said.

He pulled up a stalk of giant cane and pushed it our way,
while its mother cried and swam in circles around it. The
Dominican priest with us ran back down the mountain with
Ma. The geologist heaved the creature's smooth pink body
with its scattered hairs over to a flat rock. It was shaped
like a human moulded from badly formed clay. Its ribs were
like ours but inverted, its pinkies where our thumbs are and
its thumbs where our pinkies are. It smelled of the ocean.
Cold to the touch. Its mouth looked like it was going to say
something, or cough something out. I felt naked guilt, like
I was naked too.

No! This is not right, I said. Even my tongue was changing
and I spoke with a British accent. The geologist got a hold

45

of himself and pressed his palm against the fish. *I heard it tastes like pork fat. I just love that I see them in the flesh – their flesh, in the flesh!*

With his Bowie knife, he sliced off a square the size of a butcher's pork belly, and sliced the inner part of his own arm. He padded it on his flesh. I saw it for myself. The bleeding stopped.

I think this legendary creature is just a whale, really. They're whales.

No, sorry, it is a dugong. Pez muliers are just dugongs.

Sigh. Dugong the Dugongidae, from the family of Sirenae.

Sirena?

No, not mermaids. But a rare catch! And in freshwater! It can cure all sorts of things, and their bones can make healing rosaries. The cut that he had just made on his arm already looked like an old scar.

Soon after this incident, the geologist was dealing geckos and antiques at the seventh floor of an old office building in Hong Kong. That day I ran so fast down the mountain, then I got on a horse and galloped the short way home.

HOLY SHIT

When I woke up the next morning, the newspaper was thrown into my window tied around a stone, just missing my left temple, which woke me up with a start: *FOREIGNER AND NATIVE ACCOMPLICE KILL*

LOCAL FISHERMAN: shot him with a rifle, dragged him to the edge of the lake and cut a square of flesh from his belly. A family who were swimming at the scene witnessed the crime. The accomplice, a hirsute he/she, is from the town.

I was an apprentice tour guide. I don't know how I came to think that these creatures of myth had come alive. They say mermaid sightings make you dumb.

In 2011, two women were arrested because they were suspected of robbing a bank. They stood outside the bank prior to it opening, with four big men behind each of them. At nine, a guard whistled at the police station situated across the street. There was a shootout with the police. The women raised their handbags: a bullet ricocheted off the steel money boxes hidden inside the bags. *Don't shoot.* They were not robbing the bank. They were there to exchange a rare gecko for 5 million pesos. They were just there to kindly deposit the money. 'Kindly' is a word we always use to make demands. The police said *Yes, we can see the money; but where is the gecko?*

One of the big men standing behind them was a superintendent, who kindly asked the police that he deal with the situation himself. The cars had vehicle passes to the Palace of the President.

A circular went around: '*Geckos do not cure AIDS. They do not even cure asthma. Please stop selling golden geckos. They may not even exist.*'

Rumours went around that people living around the mountain were involved in a major tourist scam, and the whole town was in on it. Vainglory. But there were those of us who could really see the volcano – *Stop calling it the volcano*, Cowboy repeated.

He told the media that the situation was under control: *We are not on drugs – we just don't know any more what we are saying. This is just like in the south, where there is your so-called exploding land: it is not a miracle. Fields don't just explode! Take a joke. If you can't see the volcano about to – oop – neither can we. We are not all – and I speak on behalf of the town – on drugs.*

There's a lot of loot on this mountain, said the press. Whatever 'loot' stands for – Yamashita's hidden treasure or a mountain of porcelain shabu – the countryside is full of drugs, dealers, and addicts.

My neighbour's daughter was the first victim, killed by a masked motorcyclist as she lip-synced to tapes of Tiffany in front of their TV. But her mama was a drug dealer or something. She told everyone that her daughter had died tragically of cyanide poison after eating raw, unroasted cashews.

It was like Pompeii, when Pliny stood across the water at Naples, watching Mt Vesuvius erupt.

It just doesn't happen here, nobody really knows what's going on. Draw a circle around the whole town. This place is marked.

≈

Mark had a lover named Cindy who always wore outfits made out of orange shot pink taffeta. Cindy didn't want

to live in Turagsoy and so Mark told his wife Girly that he
was going to the City to meet the Interstellar Alliance. Girly
knew about Cindy, and hoped that this affair would remain
on Earth. Cindy later claimed, though no one would believe
her, that she was married to Mark.

Cindy felt that living out in the country was so boring it made
her soft. Too many sea urchins; it's all vaginas out here. In the
city, she could wear jumpsuits without getting heat rash.

Mark and Cindy were slow dancing at the Stargazer and
then after Diana Ross's 'Upside Down', the lights came
on. Mark collapsed on the pearlised tiles. *You're drunk, you
cooking banana!* Cindy tried to pull him back up with one
arm. She hadn't been with him long enough to know that
his weak heart tired easily. She had befriended the bouncer,
who allowed them to sleep with their arms crossed on the
bar to make a pillow. The janitor cleaned around them.
Cindy woke up to the smell of a cocktail carpet rather than
coffee. *Where am I*, she said, confused. *Or, where I am?*

The paradise that she had just been dancing in for hours with
air-conditioning had been transformed into a hell that was
as hot as a Turkish bath. She had no memory of the previous
evening and wanted company, so she tried to wake Mark,
but he didn't stir. His skin felt cold, so she put her cheek
next to his to cool down. She reached for his hairy nipple
to tickle him awake, and still got no reaction. She panicked.

The club's double door had been locked from the outside.
She banged and banged for an hour until a passing security
guard unlocked the door in a manoeuvre he had practiced
only seconds earlier. The double doors flew open, and he
twirled his baton and stopped its spin right at the hooligan's

nose, only to find the person in question was a woman with crimped hair like a Jesus statue, calling out for help, and that her husband needed to go to the hospital and he might be dead. The security guard said, *So, you killed him?*

No, she said, *We were only dancing.*

None of this made any sense to the watchman because they shouldn't have been in the club after closing time. *Just call an ambulance!*

Mark was taken to the nearest hospital in an ambulance. The doctor told Cindy that he had died in the emergency room, though he had really been dead for hours. He lied because he felt sorry for Cindy, who was still checking for his pulse with two fingers. In his usual open-chested tuxedo, Mark looked prepared for this moment.

The doctor asked Cindy if she was Mark's wife. The shower-curtained room that her dead lover's body rested in smelled like stale menthol cigarettes, spilled White Russians, Jack Coke, Mojito, and Pale Pilsen.

If you're not his wife then you need to get out of here. I've been told she's coming.

Cindy passed her in the hallway though they didn't spot each other. A bored doctor, upon seeing a confused Girly, her hands squeezing her head, promptly got up and signalled the nurses, and they re-enacted the performance of attempting to revive the man for the benefit of his wife.

I became aware of my situation and I began to laugh and couldn't stop, Mark's ghost said, watching as they pumped his dead body with electric current. He let out the kind of nervous laughter that came when people were all observing a moment of silence together. He was searching for any trigger – the fabric folded into the doctor's clenched buttocks, or the comically serious look of the nurse holding the cardiac defibrillator – or not even needing any, except the idea that people were straining together in a concerted effort to only make serious and necessary noises.

Cindy was, gullibly, hoping that Mark would come back to life. She wanted to believe he had been dancing tirelessly all morning, even inside the ambulance. Everybody looked so serious.

Mark found stilling silent laughter extremely difficult, and after some rest, he would start up again, and again, even if it was entirely inappropriate to do so. He had laughed throughout the entrance exams to high school and had to wanted exit the classroom to let it all out but couldn't. It was like Visconti's *The Leopard*, in the dining scene where Angelica just keeps on laughing and keeps on until the whole table is like, *Okay, well let's all proceed to the drawing room.*

Sometimes when I laugh I lose control of my thumbs. It starts around the cuticles, they become weak and it is impossible to hold things like pens, which made sitting in that exam encircling multiple choice questions very difficult. Folding my big toe becomes extremely painful. I also find that I am unable to pout, which in these parts is used to point somewhere.

Mark's ghost realised that he had never been an alien, and he was never English. He was only human.

≈

Each year, Ma would pack her bags to prepare herself for
what she called self-cleansing, a phrase that could just as well
describe taking a bath in a tub. There is a woman, they say,
who sees the Holy Mother once a year on the next mountain.
Nobody knows who, or where she's from, except maybe for
the Holy Mother. Old friends.

Ma never brought much, but she always packed a long belt
made of jingle bells that she looped several times around her
body as a safety measure, and a plastic bag for wet clothes.
Pilita needed assistance to bathe – *Kill me already, what is
this shit*, she screamed, *water?* – an impossible self-cleansing,
but as I was too unreliable, Belen had to stay behind, because,
after all, she was now family.

Why you and not me? Belen wound the jingling belt around
her waist so tightly a balloon formed around her pleated skirt,
and she stayed that way until she nearly fainted.

I need to attend, Belen protested, as they removed the triple
knots. *You don't understand.*

You can't, Ma insisted, gesturing to an invisible door and
barring it with both hands. *Because God chose me and
not you.*

Fate was constantly in the way of Ma's road to holiness,
and she was happy to acknowledge it over and again, cursing
and thanking God loudly for everyone to hear, pointing
her knowing finger like she was trying to poke a hole up
to heaven so God could hear the joke. God picked on her
exclusively, and so she wasn't obliged to do good really,

she never needed to attend mass or complete a novena, much less start one, because anyway the kind Lord would always put an obstacle before her.

The radio announced that the new president said: *When a one-year-old, an eighteen-month-old baby, is taken from a mother's arms, dragged under a jeep, raped and killed, where is God? And in Syria, women and children who don't want to have sex with ISIS, they are burned. So, where's God? My God, where are you?*

'It's God's will'. How do you know what is God's will?

Later that evening, the arowana killed itself. It allowed itself to get sucked into the filter as Ma was cleaning it, got caught and died. If the truth be told, the entire household had wanted it to die for a long time, tired of watching it circling around inside the aquarium, back and forth, back and forth, under the blue light and in the neon plastic seaweed. Still, guilt bore down on us. Pilita began to tear-up in the presence of the dead fish. It was as if the waters of the aquarium had been transferred into her eyes as we drained it. In the Feng Shui Master Yeung Bi Bi circular, it said: *You should be careful not to speak about getting rid of your arowana within earshot of it because it will commit suicide.* After realising that it was impractical to set it free, we had taken less care of it, and didn't notice that as the tank was being cleaned it often caught its tail in the filter, and so, it took its own life accidentally. Ma believes a bullet point in the circular that said that arowanas commit suicide to transfer the negative energy that enters the home into the fish instead. She asked everyone to please kindly believe this.

We have the aquarium now, so we may as well get replacement fish.

She might as well have said batteries. Jerry took everyone, including Belen, to Pet Cluster. Some small goldfish flipped over in a shallow tank next to the fish feed while he was looking at a huge waist-high tank of koi. In a shallow tray of goldfish another had flipped itself over, *Oh my god, it flipped over, Ms Saleslady, it is swimming upside down.*

The fish overate, she said.

When you eat a whole steamed fish on a plate, you don't flip it over because it's bad luck. You have to remove its translucent vertebrae to get to the other half of the fish.

Then several goldfish turned over too. The sales lady must have overfed them, and she knew she could be fired for that, and meanwhile Jerry examined the dog-size koi that he could never have in the house.

≈

I was balancing a plate of chicken to give to an old woman and her grandchild who lived in a small hut near our house. Ma told me to offer it to them with two hands. And I did, but I had developed a sense of daring that wasn't entirely mine. Ma waited behind the gate and I felt the dare challenge me, and if I didn't do it, I would die. If I failed to run past the gate and touch the doorknob of the main door before she whistled, Come in you devil, *I would die. If I didn't finish repeating* Glory Be to the Father and the Son and the Holy Spirit as It Was in the Beginning Is Now and Ever Shall Be World Without End, Amen, *five times before the end of the Nano-Nano candy commercial, I would die. Or when my godparents gave me a gift for Christmas and I was opening the gold box with the red ribbon in front of them, and they*

were smiling holding my shoulder and wearing red lipstick
that they put on just for Christmas, I must say to myself,
I hope they die. *I then gave the old woman and her*
grandchild the plate of chicken, and as I was handing it
to them, in my mind I said I hope you die. *Of course not.*
What a terrible thing to wish upon people. Of course not.
But my mind had dared me, even though it wasn't me, and
I gave it to them and I was uttering the word undo, undo.
I fear things coming true. I hope they die. I hope not. *I have*
the power to make things come true. Of course not. But now
I'd cursed them without meaning to. It's that voice! I went
upstairs and looked at them from my window and saw that
they were enjoying the meal and I worried that something
terrible was going to happen to them because of me. And
I wished that they never ate it, or that they were never
standing near our house, or that we never brushed our
yellow ramie curtains aside to check for moth wings caught
in the screen. But everything happened and I was a terrible,
terrible person and had sealed their fate. But it wasn't me,
I tried to reassure myself, it was the voice in my head daring
me to do things, to touch the doorknob ten paces away from
me before Grandmother opened her mouth to let in a big
spoon of mashed fruit. Not to open the door necessarily but
just to touch it. And if I failed, I would die. But since I always
survived, I can't prove that this can't possibly be wrong, or
that it is all in my head.

That night I couldn't sleep. It was raining and my room was
beside the gutter. The incessant downpour made my heart
beat faster, as if a water mill that powered up my anxieties
so that I drowned in them. My blanket suddenly became
extremely hot and I tossed and turned, trying to emerge
from my sweat and panic, unaware that my elbows and
my knees and the bottom of my big toe were exposed and

being devoured by mosquitos. My chest swelled as though
it too had been bitten by a mosquito – everywhere, plateaus
of red flesh that I pressed with the edge of my fingernail
to make impressions of crosses to ease the itch. And even
with the rain the chickens kept turning and turning, neither
medicinal nor magical, and – I get this tremor inside me
and I just want everything to stop. I had done this before,
I reassured myself, I had cursed Ma, Jerry, Jerry the arowana,
my godparents, my old teacher, the whole town, and nothing
had happened.

To my shock the next day I discovered that the grandmother
and the child had disappeared, and I never knew what
happened to them.

≈

Get in the confession booth, you devil. You have filled out,
Doctor Low said, and then slipped his oily black tongue
out, panting like we were in a dubbed eighties B-movie.
Saliva pooled at the tip and dripped down onto his
gabardine cassock. His hands made shapes in front of
his chest as though he were catching milk pouring out of
his nipples. It was an elaborate performance that seemed
to last forever, and a nasty smell filled the room like the
stench of unwashed laundry.

Father Low, MD, the town's parish priest, doubled as
the doctor. This was a bonus, though, not that we needed
it as there was already an entire clan of doctors available,
specialising in all parts of the body. But it came in handy to
have a priest you could confess to, and if the sin had a disease
attached to it, you got, in some way, a free consultation.
There was the man who, while watching a ping pong ball

come out of a vagina – a trick the bar owner had learned in Bangkok – had taken a hit to his open eye and got a nasty pinkeye.

Of course we'd guessed that such a talented doctor as Doctor Low claimed he was wouldn't just be a priest, and hadn't come here without a reason.

Once the whole class was forced to go carol singing and sang 'Feliz Navidad' for him while he smoked Onion cigarettes and watched from his American-style patio. *Peh-lease navedad, posporo años... Ha wanna wish you a merrrry Christmas, ha wanna wish you a merrrry Christmas, from the bottom of my heart...* And in appreciation he threw us a bag of White Rabbit candy, the soft chewy ones that don't bruise your temples when thrown at you. We liked those a lot. *Okay, that's enough, Merry Christmas, Miscreant Christmas you miscreants*, he said, and went back into his house and watched us from his kitchen jalousies. We opened the wrappers, and the soft white chews turned out to be cat poo.

He was the richest man in the entire town, and from his pulpit suspended on the right side of the church he would point at people mid-sermon – *You, you owe me money*. They said he'd been a big-time smuggler who used a fake name disappearing with cars, fabrics and other things along pre-colonial trade routes in the south. The news reported that in the water of the second largest province he'd led a band of smugglers trafficking high value contraband, using a small motor boat crammed to the gunnels with Tommy Hilfiger, cognac, and fine Puppies cigarettes.

Breath. Sometimes cigarette breath smells like a toilet, in the same way that a public restroom smells like stale underwear after a long day. Sometimes we walk over a canal and I think, the water smells like breath. Breath is heavy air, carrying the stench of the gunk you remove from the back of your mouth and from between your teeth. Or the tonsil stones – which you spit out unawares, as the detritus might be mistaken for small pieces of bitten corn or rice. Sometimes it just smells like faeces. That was the odour I caught when Dr Low tried to dance with me to *Sweet Dreams Are Made of This*. An article I read in *Woman du Jour* had advice for threatening situations, paraphrased: If you are in danger, do not 'commit your behaviour', which means don't act definitely. You can fake-faint, but really fainting commits your behaviour. If you do commit your behaviour, you lose your hold over the situation and he can do anything he wants, with his hand around your throat... So I swung my leg to *travel the world and the seven seas* instead of kicking him and forcing his shin backwards, and raised both arms to *let the joy rise into the ocean* instead of ramming my palm against the front of his neck.

You have filled out, Doctor Low repeated.

You mean since I was standing outside?

You dry little urchin. You have a devel... a devil-opmental problem.

A Jerry problem, Ma shouted from outside, surprised that people expected a curtained wooden booth to possess a sufficient level of privacy.

Ma had delivered me, her little devil, to Dr Low, pulling my left arm with both of hers, which was a dramatic move since it was far easier just to pull a person along with one arm, and, anyway, there was no resistance. *This child...*

Sir, I'm legal, I said.

… has the compulsion to call whatever's in sight 'Jerry', she told him.

How did it start, asked the Doctor.

How did it start, growled Ma.

I have always remembered that Ma, in this moment, worried and spiteful with sweat on her lips (she had no philtrum) and her two curled feet scraping the floor, had no idea what the answer was, and in her agitation had started to bite the hair that had fallen into her mouth from a rotating fan on 3. This was to remain my most important memory of her.

They say Dr Low, who had no wrinkles at the age of ninety-two, was the missing Tomas Limo, an old smuggler of the nineteen-fifties who, when captured, nobody seemed to know what to do with because they couldn't easily classify him as a criminal or a citizen. He was born here, he said, and had worked as an intelligence agent for the government. Others said his aliases included Tomas Bata, who was a Chinese citizen, only there was no record of his coming in – *a spy for Communist China!* Bata smuggled contraband goods and undocumented migrants. *That alien!* said the government. And while they were all figuring him out, they let him go. Interest died down and he escaped forever.

Where did 'Jerry' come from, Dr Low asked, as if explaining Jerry was a way to get rid of him.

It came from Jerry, of course, Ma said.

Who is Jerry?

Tomas! I yelled, as he walked towards the room beside
the altar.

Dr Low turned around.

≈

At Congregate, a retreat situated on an elevation up from
the driveway that made it appear like a halfway home to the
heavenly kingdom, my mother, Maggie, Lilibeth, and Letty
always took room 121. It had one king-sized bed and a private
ensuite bathroom for four people. They talked about their
children until they said their prayers together at midnight,
holding hands, excited that they were scheduled to wake up
in just a few hours to witness a miracle. Their sleeping gowns
were floral, and sleeping together they looked like a flower
bed. On a floor right below them, unpacking her brown pleat
dress, was the woman who could see the Holy Mother.

Are you still awake?

I was sleeping. I'm awake now.

I wanted to tell you that there was a plot to kill Father Low.

Now you're scaring me, how can I sleep?!

Father Low smuggled...

No!

Which was fine, but he...

*For the sake of His sorrowful passion, for the sake of His
sorrowful passion...*

And so, he pissed off...

*For the sake of His sorrowful passion, for the sake of His
sorrowful passion!*

And so, he will be...

*I'm so scared now, so scared now. I'm so scared of what
you're saying I need to drown it out. I need to stick my
fingers in my ears and shake them, I need to rattle my ears
to drown out the sound. I need you to stop talking. I need
you to let me sleep. My imagination is going wild. I can't
stop it. I can't get the images out of my mind.*

*Okay, change topic. Stop hu-hu-ing. I'll tell you something
I read yesterday. Centuries ago there was a native widow
from Dapitan who applied to join a Catholic convent. She
gave all her possessions away to her children in order to
ready herself to become a nun. To 'revirginise,' you could
say. But because she was a native, she wasn't allowed into
the Spanish convent – even, as she begged, just as a slave.
And so, she cloistered herself inside her own house. They
say she was a leader in a battle – revenge I guess, or maybe
more for freedom, I don't know if it was before or after
the self-seclusion, or the rejection. They called her Maria
Uray, or Virgin Mary, and allegedly she still lives in a cave
to this day.*

Do you think this is Macabebe Marie?

No, this was in the Muslim south, in the sixteen hundreds.

Do you think she re-emerged as Macabebe Marie?

*I'm so scared now. I hate you. I hope you die, I wish
you death.*

What?

Sorry, I don't know where that came from.

They set out for the mountain at four the next afternoon,
supporting their marbled thighs on bignay trees and bamboo
bridges as they climbed upwards. Ma was angry that her
alarm clock hadn't woken her up and she had to be shaken
from her sleep yelling and everyone was waiting for her
in the lobby cursing. She was not happy with the Lord.

*You know I was thinking about that thing you said,
about Maria Uray coming back as Macabebe Marie...*

For the sake of His sorrowful passion...

*You know I bought a book by Joan Grant... She wrote
those* Far Memory *books where she described her past lives...*

Yeah, I heard about that.

*I'm scared again. If I had my way I would crucify you for
constantly scaring me and for bringing up things I don't want
to hear...*

As ships heading for Mexico passed Batangas, sailors would
shoot into the air, as a salute to the Lady of Cagsaysay,
for a safe journey. Once, a fleet of Chinese pirates came
to Batangas and tried to vandalise her shrine, and the Lady

appeared as an apparition. One of the pirates lunged at her face and struck at her cheek...

They finally reached the top of the mountain where rocks have been set in a circle, a small amphitheatre below an acacia tree where the woman they called Marian could speak to the mother Mary.

Ten days before Christmas, the day of the prom, Jerry strained hot vinegared milk into a clump of cheese that swelled like a brain and everyone at the table – me, Jerry, Pilita – said *cheers and long life*. Shortly afterwards, we all vomited right beneath the Christmas tree and the puke seeped under the hardwood floorboards while Ma and Belen were away seeing Mary.

There was a man on a Friday afternoon news segment explaining that calculus came from the Kerala school in India, and was not from the West. *But though these scholars disappeared, we will always have curry*, he said. Namaste, and Merry Christmas.

There was silence before the main radio broadcaster spoke again. *Sometimes you have to be really good friends with someone to realise you are really strangers.*

The Marian Seer spoke an ancient Greek dialect that was familiar to St John the Baptist and similar to the language deployed by Emma de Guzman, so heavily accented that it was difficult to tell it apart from Shakespeare... She witnessed a shower of rose petals, with each fleshy pad carrying images from Heaven, like the apparition in Lipa in 1949. Although it was evening the Seer saw the dancing sun, similar to what Angel de la Vega – once known as Judiel Nieva – saw on Apparition Hill in 1989... (But *her* apparitions were discredited by the church, it seems, because of moral turpitude – *she was transsexual*, they said, ignoring other matters such as the statue of Mother Mary in her house that may have been crying pig's blood and that all the money supposedly donated for the construction of a church had never broken ground…)

After she received a pailful of holy water she recovered her senses. Smiling, she said that she had seen the Infant Jesus lying in a manger. *But what does the manger look like?*

And she said, *Ah well, you know it was a bamboo hut, it was made of straw and bamboo like a belen. In fact, all the animals were so cute in the nativity scene they looked like they were just cast figurines of donkeys, cows, and sheep.*

Kneeling, the Marian Seer fell into a trance. Light from petroleum lamps held at the top of bamboo sticks formed irregular shadows. A man sold handkerchiefs with an imprint of the Seer's face on it, like the Holy Shroud, with real gold edging along the sides. *Come, come, cower, come, not worthy, cower*, were the words that could be heard. The rest were a vulgar Latin, which to the women present could have easily been French, and then suddenly, like a contestant who wins a car, she yelled with joy, *Holy Mother, I am here to witness you.*

People looked around and there was nothing. They didn't see anything but they believed, they had blind faith. They heard a cracking sound and everybody gasped, as gold frost came down and ziploc bags and clutch purses were opened to receive it, and the escarchas, which they called 'the frost', stuck to Belen's tears like glitter on clear Elmer's glue. Ma recognised the Seer, and fainted. *Fuck the King!*

The group began their descent down the mountain holding the golden frost tight under their armpits, like the chickens on the spit.

Meanwhile in front of the television watching the Marian miracle live, as there was nothing much to see except kerosene lamps in the darkness, Jerry had a heart attack.

You should go back to the house. Your blind date is coming.

The town's evening gala was held on the day of Jerry's death. Leaving the ossuary behind the church to attend the dance wasn't difficult. While sorting out the funeral arrangements on her own, Ma had felt for the outline of Jerry's forehead beneath a floral green sheet. *I'll avenge your death,* she said, crying, and I said, *How do you avenge a heart attack?*

The dress was hanging behind the main door. The straps of the dress were so long that I had to push my shoulders up to reach it. Bert my prom date was late because he thought the entire family was in the morgue.

Sorry for your loss. How are you? I'm fine thank you, and *it's good to meet you. So, you're okay? Yeah, it was a tragic.* By reframing it into a noun: 'a tragic,' as opposed to 'a tragic accident' or 'a tragedy,' it appeared commonplace, less startling, more just a type of radio code: It was a tragic, ten-four, go go. He held out a gift, a doll which mechanically repeated *weh, weh,* and then *weh, weh,* until you burped her by flicking a switch on her back. He asked me to dance to *Sweet Dreams Are Made of This.*

≈

Right after Christmas we buried Jerry, and Ma put away
her jingle bell belt for the year. She sold our entire porcelain
collection and used the glass counter to showcase various
trinkets, including necklaces made of escarchas, ceramic
nativity sets, and 'Belen's Tears,' and then put Belen in an
air-conditioned room with a permanent veil. The family had
Angus steak for the first time. It was well done. *Happy New
Year!* Ma shot Saucisson because he was old and wounded
and she had lost interest in chickens, and then she regretted
it because someone offered to partner her in an expansion.

The bishops and a cardinal named Sin who came to visit
Belen did not accept that she had any holy powers, although
she used to descale fish, and her black rubber loafers would
suddenly sparkle with sequins. *They weren't merely fish*, Ma
said in English. Ma had been told that 'merely' was a word
you used on important occasions and elevated the tone of
English conversation. 'Only' did not have the same effect.

≈

I applied for a job at the local radio station.

Do you have any experience in voice acting?

*Yes. I like to modulate my voice to be heard at certain angles
from the hilltop*, I told them.

You have a very interesting voice, she said. *Very adaptable,
it sounds both very low and high, almost as if two people
are speaking at once. It could be good for horrors, choruses,
or market scenes.*

I am a tour guide of my home, our home, the great volcano.
I specialise in re-enactment, ma'am.

Can you read this for me?

Hide now all the children and don't get caught by The
Lady Pig in Clogs. Don't get caught because she will eat
you. Here she comes now the Lady Pig in Clogs. I am coming
down the street now, clog, clog, clog, clog. Oh no, let's hide.
Clog, clog, clog. Where are the children now? Oh no! Clog,
clog, clog, I have found a child now. Clog, clog, clog, clog.
I have reached the child now. I will eat the child now.

Now, say it once more. With feeling.

≈

That all happened too quickly. Perhaps the arowana did have
magical powers, and in order to receive good luck, everyone
in the house had to eat the pet fish that had been preserved
in the freezer. Maybe Ma should sell arowana, but not as
aquarium fish: she could descale, clean, flour, fry, and wrap
it in banana leaf. Price it at a premium as fortune fish with
auspicious pak choy on the side.

She opened a case with the Bureau of Aquatic Resources
and Fisheries for the arowana to be farmed for food.
Alongside it, she would also serve regular market fish
to address the psychology of those who would never ask
for the most expensive thing on a menu and instead get
whatever's next cheapest. Second-rate fish would make
most of the money. Nobody had done this before. There
was no economic precedent for a business like this. This
was innovation.

Each morning, Ma would clean the fish with a serrated knife which sent the scales flying. She was used to chickens, not fish, and cut herself many times on a protruding dorsal fin. The sponge was covered in scales, the drain was covered in scales, the handle of the sink was covered in scales, her hair had scales, the cat food had scales. It was hard to tell the difference between fingernails and scales. Everything became about scales. Scales are strange. Does a fish feel pain if its scales are removed before it dies? Can snakes and lizards be descaled? A fish the wholesaler sold us was half-defecating a large fat turd the size of a flower stem.

The most important and most secret part of Ma's new occupation was that she would collect the scales, and then send them to the local chemist to make glitter.

≈

They said his shoes had convinced voters that he would be an honest President. He didn't need to steal money because as he walked, his left heel talked. It flew open like a crocodile's mouth. But if he walked his talk…

Larry Hillblom, the founder of the DHL empire, the 'H', had similar footwear. He used to come to these parts. Jerry once sat across from him in a hotel bar, *What a man*, he said, blond in his blue jeans but one of the richest men in the world.

Eh? I'm just a pilot from Saipan, he had told Jerry. *Why do you ask? I come to Manila because I like to lie down and look at the stars.*

When I saw the girls fawning over him I knew he wasn't just some regular guy…

It was said that Hillblom used to keep mama-sans fat with cash so that they would supply him with virgins as young as thirteen. *I just like to look at the stars*, he said. One day he took an old plane and disappeared forever in the skies of Saipan.

There were lawsuits but there was no Hillblom to take the paternity tests. They supposedly poured muriatic acid over the sink and buried his comb and toothbrush in his backyard and, according to the *Wall Street Journal*, not even the facial mole a San Francisco hospital had removed could be used. They did a sibling DNA test for Junior, Jellian, Mercedita, and Lory – all pointing to the conclusion that despite living islands apart, they had perhaps been fathered by the same man.

They each earned $90 million dollars before tax. The eldest, Junior Larry Hillbroom (the spelling on his birth documents was an error), owner of his father's luxury resorts, tried to dive into the sea to escape charges of 'ice trafficking' in Palau.

≈

In the 1987 movie *Ang Mga Anak ni Facifica Falayfay*, comedians Dolphy, Babalu, and Panchito play cops in the drug squad. They are ushered into the Mayor's office. There is a cowboy hat on the desk.

Dolphy: *Oh, the mayor went out. He left his hat.*

The hat suddenly moves and the mayor appears from under the desk.

Mayor: *I dropped my ball pen.*

He asks Pacifico Manalastas, played by Dolphy, to sit down.

Mayor: *I called you here because we have a big problem in our city, and our country, because of illegal drugs. I want you to take out the heads of the syndicates.*

Pacifico: *Rest assured Mr Mayor we will catch the queen of the termites in our country.*

The next scene is an award ceremony.

Sergeant: *...and the National Police Efficiency Medal is hereby awarded to Pacifico Manaslatas!*

A young man, Rodrigo, played by Roderick Paulate, goes on stage in a tight pink shirt and white stockings and does a special number.

Rodrigo: *Daddy-o, this is for you...*

The speakers play Paul Lakakis's *Boom Boom (Let's Go Back to My Room).*

Later at home, Pacifico confronts Rodrigo.

Rodrigo: *Daddy why?!*

Pacifico: *How dare you I was being given an award earlier and you put me to shame! You even flirted with the mayor!*

Rodrigo: *But Dad, you get mad so easily. I was only trying to make you happy! I surprised you!*

Pacifico: *What surprise – I was FLUMMOXED! From now on, we will go back to the way it used to be. I'll make you a man.*

Rodrigo: *Ay! But Daddy! I don't want to be a man!*

Pacifico hits him with a wok and his entire body vibrates. We dissolve into next scene:

Rodrigo is wearing military fatigues doing drill commands, and is punched in the ass by his brother as he gyrates.

Rodrigo: *What's your problem!*

Rodrigo's Brother: *Can't you make yourself stiffer? More macho…*

Rodrigo: *That was stiff already!*

Rodrigo's Brother: *That was stiff already?*

Rodrigo: *That was stiff already! And anyway I'm not macho, and then you beat me up but I'm the only teenage girl in this family!*

Later that evening, Rodrigo is lying down on a chaise sofa with hair clips around his head, looking up at a portrait of his mother, played by Zsa Zsa Padilla, who resembles Imelda Marcos. Rodrigo cries to the painting: *Naku, Mami, bukas oombagin ako. Chuchugi-chugihin na naman nila ang beauty ko. Pinipilit nila ako maging 'mean'. E hindi naman ako 'mean', Diba? Alam mo naman yun e! Mami! Bahala ka na. (Oh no, Mommy, tomorrow they will clobber me. They will stab-stab my beauty again. They're forcing me to become 'mean'. But I'm not 'mean', right mommy? You know that! Mommy! I leave it up to you.)*

Rodrigo is dreaming. He is still wearing his Minnie Mouse T-shirt. The landscape around him is gravelly. His father and two brothers appear as three aliens trying to grab hold

of him. He begs for mercy as he is about to be thrown over
a cliff. His grandmother comes to his rescue and threatens
to kill the men.

Grandmother: *I'll shoot you between the eyes!*

She blasts purple lasers at them with her cane.

Men in the family: *We don't feel anything!*

Grandmother: *You don't feel pain?*

She is wearing a papier-mâché island for a hat. Rodrigo's
mother appears suddenly beside his grandmother to help save
him, but immediately they are both lassoed with a white laser.
The men are shoving Rodrigo into a spacecraft the size of
a small elevator. A red snapper flies off the grandmother's
large yellow 'island' hat and shoots through the machine.
The men of the family push Rodrigo in. They shut the door
as his mother screams. The men rush to the control panel
and flick the 'sex change' lever. They press several other
buttons. A flash of light indicates that the process has begun.
First, Rodrigo appears as a mermaid with gold-painted
nipples, flirtatiously flapping his purple tail. There is
a light-coloured appendage much like a skinned banana
on his tail. His father pushes more buttons in the control
panel. Rodrigo pushes the door open to reveal that he has
become a shrieking sea monster, or 'siokoy'. He is green,
with netting for scales. He chases after the men with his
green hands. He strangles his father, and then he wakes up.

Siokoys are mythical monsters that come out of the water
and are considered to be merfolk. Coco and Therese from
the admin department of the municipal hall have issued

a circular to clarify that siokoys are people suffering from harlequin-type ichthyosis, and find it is soothing to immerse their bodies in water.

≈

In a television interview Belen said that at one point in her life, she had lost everything and just sat inside a church not knowing what to do. Her wallet had been emptied by a teenage gang. Out of boredom, they had extracted devil's breath from the (widely grown) angel's trumpet bushes around the church grounds. She was under their spell. After being drugged and robbed she woke up lying on the steps of the altar, at the lowest point in her life. She had walked aimlessly behind the church and had her first Marian vision, which was cruder than later manifestations, because she saw the face of the Mother Mary in the bark of a jackfruit tree. Mary spoke to Belen. When Belen was accused on television of being a manipulative drunk, she turned to the camera with hurt eyes, and said that those who spoke ill of her would never enter the Promised Land that she had seen in her visions.

Belen was wearing a dark ramie blouse that looked like a visual representation of static noise. It is a pattern usually associated with buildings from the eighties – office lobbies enamelled with brown-tinted glass and patched together with a pervasive ochre marble, where the plumbing fixtures are moulded beige, and the chrome taps look like a small penis or a prepuce, and they are difficult to twist open without getting your fingers dirty on the uncleaned sink.

All attention in the house was focused on Mary and Baby Jesus. Foot-washing became an initiative of Belen's, who said it was what Jesus did to sinners.

*Like you, you are a sinner because you listen to punk bands.
What did you learn from punk bands?*, she asked me.

*Nothing, just enjoyed listening to them on a Bugs Bunny
Sony Discman.*

Powder cake Lucifer!

I was slapped across the face like a pounder smashing
a clove of garlic! Belen, seeking penance, looked down
howling, caressing her breasts as if ants had crawled into
her bra – then she yanked her shirt collar down, covered
her hands with it, and extracted a small rose from between
her ribcage. The corsage was sealed with blood and mucus.
She placed it on my lap. And then out came another.
And then another. I ran.

*That is pain, that is the pain of beauty, when it encounters
the flesh of sin. Yes, go on! Get out of here!*

Nobody believed me when I told them what happened,
except Ma, who had raised her eyebrow and said that she was
very glad to hear that. The next year, at the annual mountain
gathering, roses came out of Belen's body, and Ma sold
distilled bottles of alkaline rose water in the thousands.

Belen described the barnyard shelter this way: Two sheep
on the left, one donkey standing in the centre, and a cow
on the right. The positions of the animals were copied from
the porcelain nativity scene in the house. Ma built herself
a storage room and disappeared into it with Belen. Their
shoes were always covered with flecks of gold frost. They
scared off anyone who dared to look in the direction of
Belen's house, because the angels were keeping her safe.

Can you see the angels too? they asked me.

No. Got no such special powers. I'm just a sacristan servant of the Lord.

You are a sacristan? They asked in disbelief.

I looked down at my chest. I could see my heart muscles twitching as if they were winking at me. Eventually I began to work inside the storage workshop, with a cleaver and a pounder, helping to make the gold frost.

In the hours that the devotees waited for her to speak, Belen often fell asleep. And in that sleep she dreamt of a long war, and in that war, there was a man with a buzz cut tying up a velvet curtain because he thought it was ugly.

That night a woman was screaming outside the house. She kept it up for so long that it drove the dogs wild. Usually the neighbours' mongrels only barked madly at the sound of sexual climax. But tonight, all the dogs on the street were barking as the woman outside kept screaming. *Maybe the old lady and her granddaughter are outside, maybe the old lady and the granddaughter want to kill everyone. Maybe it's Ma. Maybe it's the neighbour.* A black butterfly entered through the hole in the screen door. *Go, you butterfly, go to the seventh mountain!* yelled Ma, holding an electric mosquito-killing plastic racket. The insect disappeared with a blue spark. The next day, Ma discovered the screaming woman was a pig with large balls.

A representative of the Church came to the Pet Centre where everyone was gathered and announced that there were no supernatural phenomena on the hill. Belen was not home.

That day, the police kicked the double doors open, though I told them they were unlocked, and arrested Ma for producing fake miraculous goods. She waved at me and Grandma Pilita from the van. It was not sentimental…

≈

Two columns of Italian green marble embellished the entrance to the old bungalow DWWZ 666. I arrived on a temperate morning. I was forced to push aside a large clump of violet bougainvillea to get to the door. Its shadow cast black fingers over the entire structure. The bush was so large it made the entire façade dark, as if it was shrouded in the night. A lone protruding branch reached over to flick the privates of everyone who passed the narrow entrance. A man had the windows open to clean them, so the reflection I saw was a glass pane of pure green hedge. The thick cairn steps were high and ridged like a clamshell, so getting to the entrance below the acrylic signage 'Radi-O my God! : DWWZ 666', became a strangely difficult ascent. This entrance had been built in such thick-set concrete, from tympanum to banister, that it appeared to be a separate structure to the rest of the building. In the back, a bungalow made of old plywood and patched up where the condenser units reminded visitors that the station had experienced better years. The entrance looked like a shrine, an entry into itself. So, when I walked into the station proper and sat at reception I felt I was somewhere else.

A news programme was wrapping up. *None of the Senators should talk*, said the committee chairman Dick Goto. *Nobody watching should open their mouth. As they say in Spanish,* 'En boca cerrada no entran moscas,' *meaning, 'Don't open your mouth or a fly might get in.'*

The studio manager asked me to sit next to him. The control board looked to me like an abacus. I was very careful with my elbows.

This station operates with a delay on its live broadcasts.

How long, sir?

It could be months.

Hello? I greeted the microphone.

The station manager knocked his head on the control board. The VU metre twitched.

Hello? I repeated again, embarrassed. I had nothing prepared.

I was moved to the production studio to narrate the life story of Belen, a pious Marian in the lineage of Veronica Lueken and Emma de Guzman. Belen had disappeared two years ago. Dwindling numbers of devotees had struggled to climb the mountain they had once charged up in the rain, and those who did so lamented that they could no longer hear Our Lady's message. Belen had climbed atop a tall rock to take the hand of a floating apparition, as from heaven, she exclaimed, she could better broadcast messages to the world in our language. She looked over at her audience of seven once more before she dived off the edge of the rock, down into the roots of the tall trees. Though really, no one can be sure where she went.

Since 1970, Our Lady of the Roses, as she was called, had been appearing to a woman named Veronica Lueken from New York. It happened on the Feast of Our Lady, September

8, which marks the birth of Mary. It was raining on the vigil, which lasted from after dinner to midnight. People had been making their way to the Vatican Pavilion in the World's Fair grounds in Queens.

It truly rains teardrops from Heaven. It is for the protection of all, their human needs, their human bodies – that we send upon you this heavy rainfall. I assure you my children, you will understand that none can climb onto roofs when the rain is falling upon them... Know that you will not become ill from these heavenly drops. Hundreds of people were drenched in the rain, ushered in by Lueken's White Berets, voluntary diehards, all of whom wished to catch a glimpse of another Mary, who – Lueken, now looking at the Holy Mother, suffused with heavenly light – was white and slender with roses on her feet and wore golden sandals. The entire vista, she said, was a shade of pink never seen on Earth.

I admonish you about this diabolical machine – the television – for you may consider it as a mechanical agent of Satan now, but in the future, my child, it will be used to brainwash your children into submission to evil.

Pope Pius XII proclaimed St. Clare of Assisi to be the Patron Saint of Television, in 1957, because she was once bedridden and unable to attend mass, so the Holy Spirit brought images and sound to her room.

Turagsoy received the news of Lueken through a woman from Rougemont, Quebec who had compiled all these messages, 290 in all, and shipped them all in a cardboard box in the name of prevailing faith. Pilita has kept them all, stored neatly beneath the television, that diabolical machine, because we found that we enjoyed cable.

In March 1983, Our Lady of Roses Veronika narrated
of the assassination of John Paul II, who has been the face
of our kitchen calendar when not alternated with the singer
Jose Mari Chan.

*I see a man. He's dressed as a cleric, the clergy. He has in
his left hand a knife. It's a long knife – no, it's like a sabre...
I don't know... he's pulling it out of his pants. It seems to
be in his pant leg near his belt. And it's very long. And he's
pulling it out with his left hand and starting to raise it, and in
his right hand he has a revolver, a small gun – not a shotgun,
a small gun. And he's screaming, and everything has become
silent about him with the screams 'Death to the Pope! Death
to the Pope!'*

*Now for the mellow sounds of Taylor Deane, with 'Love
Will Lead You Back'.*

My chest folded inwards, and I had to breathe quickly
with my stomach expanding, pumping in, pumping out;
and each time I worried that the message that Mother Mary
had sent through to Veronica on September 11, 1990, and
in January 1991, may have predicted 9/11: *Refrain from
any 'foreign' travel, especially within the New York and
Washington D.C. area...* I am afraid of airplanes and I could
not read further. I was unable to sleep because the world
is overcome with sin and I worried that *I am a child who
does not realise that I have been conquered by Satan and
the illuminati* and I worried that *I am already overcome
with wickedness...* Teeming with it – 'teeming' is a word
I associate with insects – because transgression is all around
me and in my brain, and I had not heeded the message of
Veronika Lueken or ever used our cable subscription to
watch the station EWTN.

1991 brought the arrival of Emma de Guzman into the
Marian stratosphere. Outside a church in Singapore she
saw a whirlwind carrying a pamphlet that would take her
to Ontario. She then went to New York to see the Our
Lady of Fatima shrine. *In heaven, there are a lot of mansions,*
she said, that each housed a variety of religions. *As long as
we follow, we will all go to heaven. Do you believe me?*

Yes! (In chorus.)

That's the truth, that's the truth.

She also claimed that Jesus came to her disguised as a
beggar...

In the 1941 adaptation of *Ibong Adarna*, three princes set
off, as in the tale, to find a mythical bird that could save the
life of their sick father, the king of Berbanya. The prince who
successfully caught the bird would replace him as king. They
set off to the mountain of Tabor to find the ibong Adarna.

The first Prince came across a beggar who asked for bread.
He didn't want to offer him his lunch; the journey from
castle to mountaintop looked like a one-day affair. He
reached the magical tree and then waited for evening when
the ibong Adarna would roost. Finally, the bird arrived
and began to sing. It sang an operatic melody. The bird they
got for it had a long tail that looked like feather pants worn
by a ventriloquist's dummy. The director may have cast
a pheasant for the role. The prince fell asleep beneath
the bird. After singing seven times, the bird defecated on
the prince, which turned him to stone. The second brother
undertook the same journey and experienced the same
petrifaction.

Finally, the third and youngest, Príncipe Juan, came upon the beggar and gave him something to eat. The bread used in this film was a large roll. It looked like an enlarged hamburger bun, but bigger so that you needed two hands to hold it. It appeared slightly under-baked and was smooth like a baby's butt. Later in a cave, the beggar reappeared to give Principe Juan back his bread. He also gave the youngest prince important instructions: *Do not fall asleep when the bird sings. Here are some limes to keep you awake. Avoid the droppings that come after the singing. Contact with the bird's faeces will turn you to stone. Here's some water to douse on the stone slabs beneath the roosting tree to bring your brothers back to life.*

In the original story, the two princes had simply chanced upon the tree. It was called 'Piedras Platas', or 'Silver Stones', because it shimmered. They say that Emma de Guzman's escarchas, found in trees, are of the same phenomenon.

Lueken claims to have seen an apparition of Jesus wearing slippers by the tallest tree. She tells her followers of an urgent message, dated June 18, 1994:

You will continue, My children, with the prayers of atonement. And I must tell you the time is, in Earth time, growing short. There will be a great Chastisement sent upon mankind. You will recognise this when you find in the atmosphere a huge, immense ball of light. Do not be affrighted, My child. Your scientists will be bewildered. It is the little people who will know the truth. Now, My child, you will sit back and rest. But remember, the message to the world is urgent. I do not want to place upon you, My child, the burden of knowing the full results.

Has it happened? Has it metaphorically happened? The Earth is a huge ball of fire. Is the Earth going to destroy itself? Is it war? Is it the volcano that is about to…

About to… It's gonna… I need to…

… make more of an effort to stay conscious. Sudden low blood sugar. Sometimes I must make sure that my soul doesn't leave my body. I would prefer to be lightheaded than unable to contain my own soul… My palms perspired and sweat broke out in a halo around my scalp. I stood by an open door where a man was cleaning the windows. We did not speak.

The only air-conditioning in the building was inside the recording studio, and the artificial cold always activated the lactic acid in my knees so that they squeaked as I walked around. Soft cone cladding protruded from the walls of the soundproof booth, and looked like a checkerboard from some angles. Fred, the actor beside me, wore ragged socks with his sliders, and his middle toe protruded through a big hole. It was extremely vulgar. As I stood waiting my turn, the pattern of the soundproofing began to swell and warp while the talk was wrapping up. I prevented myself from exiting my body.

Applause brought me back to consciousness. They liked my sample reading. I told everyone that re-enacting the disappearance of Belen was a very personal journey for me. *I may need to warn you that I would never deliver as good a performance again. I am nervous, very nervous.*

Why?

Because I knew Belen, she was my aunt.

She was everyone's aunt, darling.

Fred and Tony stuck out their tongues and wrote the
alphabet in the air. Their breath was indistinguishable
from microphone foam. Stretch it, they said. Like this.
And intonate. The nine-thirty to ten programme was
the end of their shift. Everybody in the cast was chopping
paper on a high podium and bleating like goats. Then
suddenly, the rest of the actors stood in position, zipped
and blank-faced, but I was seated. And so, we began
the dramatisation of Belen –

Sorry, sorry, said the station manager. *On the eve of the
anniversary of his death, and as a tribute to a dear friend,
we must do the dramatisation of the Macabebes first,
written by a certain Mr Banawan, an old friend, dear
old friend and confidante… If only to hear the sound
of the piano track again…*

The assistant comes in – *Shh!* – and is given a sheet of
a script: *Diego Salvador and the Macabebes.* The booth
seemed to swell again. It flashed at the sides as I began to
listen. I was falling through the wooden backing of the bench,
through the egg carton cones, through the drywall partition,
through the cement floor and into the thick forest where
I was to await the coming of the Macabebes…

*Before the arrival of Magellan in the archipelago, mapped
by Pigafetta as a clump of brownish islands, and long before
national consciousness arose, there existed a constellation
of established Mohammedan kingdoms. Almost fifty
years later, having explored the world and in the spirit
of conquest, the Spaniards returned to seize land from all
the chiefs and the Sultanates of ancient lineage with gifts*

*of gold, and failing that, by force. There was one ruler of
the Macabebe who refused to yield to the pacification and
repression that Miguel Lopez de Legazpi wrought in 1571.*

Cue the jungle sounds, which, due to budget limitations,
are only the sounds of crickets. They were loud!

The mighty kingdom of Macabebe declared war...

Datu Tarik Soliman: *May the sun strike me in twain,
and may I fall in disgrace before the women, who would
hate me if I ever became, for a moment, a friend to
the Castilians.*

*...and attacked the Spanish parrots, clang! lak! But the
Spanish had come to subdue them with ammunition and
hired archers from Visayas. Thwoot! Thwoot! Araaaayyyyy,
ku, leader Datu Tarik Soliman is felled!'*

*Surrender! Klak. Those fierce Macabebes left alive: surrender
to the Spanish! We surrender, we surrender...and give you
our arms and dedicate our lives to your service, and from
that point, become the best native fighters for Mama España.*

Conveniently, for the conquerors, the Macabebes had long
hated the Tagalogs. Many years ago, the nearby kingdom
of the Tagalogs invited the highest of the Macabebe men
to partake in a meal. The Macabebes were delighted by
the invitation. They set off, and, after two nights and a day,
reached the land of the Tagalogs. A stone's throw away.
It was a convivial meeting, and then, as they sat around in
circles, the mighty Tagalogs pulled up their chins to reveal
vulnerable throats. *Klllllllllk.* The Macabebes never forgot
this hospitality.

It was very unfortunate, then, that Diego Salvador, leader of the revolution, was Tagalog.

Although often delayed, newspapers regularly reached Palanan.

Salvador: *I have had the amusing experience of reading, on several occasions, reports of my own death, and subsequently a detailed account of an imaginary adventure in Cavite last December, in which I was said to have only very narrowly escaped being captured.*

For Spain, the Macabebes fought against the Chinese pirate Limahong, and then invaded the Chinese quarters in Manila and massacred the Chinese, a job that made the Spanish call them the most civilised of the native groups. Later, they were used by the Spanish in Borneo, Japan, and China, although these attempts at colonial expansion failed. Spain, a thwarted hegemony, whose own colonies – Cuba and our young nation – were to rise up in revolt. The British, who also tried to conquer our home turf, exclaimed that the Macabebes were so fierce that they gnawed at bayonets!

As the revolutions erupted, a thoroughly weakened Spain sold our land to the US for peanuts. The US had promised independence to our fledgling nation, but instead decided, *no*. Blaming the savage Tagalogs for killing their red-faced sons, the US needed native land forces to save any more of their boys from getting killed, so the Macabebes, excellent terrain warriors, became their mercenaries too.

The Macabebe Scouts, with high cheekbones and long hair, wore American khaki pants, blue gingham shirts, bamboo hats with blue felt bands and a brass eagle emblem. Their

Krag-Jorgensen carbines were slung over their shoulders. They folded their khaki pants high up to their knees to walk miles in the rain. The Americans couldn't keep up with them even if they were riding ponies. The Scouts carried rice in their socks, which they also draped over their shoulders. They were tougher fighters than the Americans could ever be. They became part of the regular army – even though they were only paid half what the yanquí soldiers received, and in Mexican dollars, not in gold. They were not afraid of anyone and they frightened everyone else. They had been setting fire to Tagalog villages when General Batson got permission to make them scouts.

Diego Salvador asked his trusted courier Manuel Paso-Paso, an Ilocano aide and former Spanish policeman who later joined the revolution, to carry a letter:

Salvador: *Make sure these are sent straight to my cousin and a few officers. I need more reinforcements and supplies.*

Starved from nearly a month of jungle travel, Paso-Paso found the Americans and surrendered to them in exchange for a $300 reward.

Paso-Paso helped forge a reply from a General Lacuna, with news of incoming reinforcements including some map-making American prisoners of war, and commending Lieutenant Colonel Placido and the Spaniard Lieutenant Ejercito for promotion.

About eighty Macabebe Scouts, disguised either in the formal blue and white uniforms of the insurgents or in plain tattered clothing, were on a gunboat called the Vicksburg. They had the American prisoners of war.

Macabebes: *We are all on a boat! Can I have some caffee, Mister? Wishwishwishwish.*

American: *I miss American rations... Cracked corn, yecch...*

The sound of their hair as it blew against the wind like flags...

Macabebes: *We want blood!* [Panting.]

Records say that they loved carving out the shapes of honeycombs, using a knife, their teeth and rough surfaces.

Land-ho!

The Macabebes reached the shore of Dibacal. There are some six miles of rough terrain before they reached the remote town of Palanan, where Salvador was being kept.

Macabebes: *We are now climbing out of the ship, with Mauser and Remington rifles, Krags, and our five American captives. Wink. Prisoners of war...*

Ever since he was a child, Salvador had been afraid of velvet. It looked like liquid to him – a thick viscous liquid turned solid so that it could be shaped into the lining inside precious boxes. When he was a child, he was given a slice of velvet by an uncle who imported goods from the old world, and it was like nothing he'd ever played with before. It was almost clotted, like the blood of a chicken on rice. It made his saliva taste bitter and made him wretch. It was disgusting, like doilies crocheted out of hair or affixed to dresses to cover the bosom. He could not bear the sight, and ran under the skirt of his mother. After using her skirt as a tent and handkerchief, he noticed she was wearing red velvet slippers. He ran off in tears, and as he did so he knocked over several kerosene lamps. When he rushed back, he heard his mother yelling, *Help, Help*. Now, he was faced with velvet again and it gave him a sense of foreboding.

Salvador: *How garish that the new drapery is velvet! Burn it tonight!*

The boy, and the rest of the town, had spent weeks searching for the best and most luxurious curtains to protect his employer from the heat. They were a special birthday present, but now he was afraid to say so.

Many people believed Salvador was protected by a kapre, a cigar-smoking mythical giant. It lived outside the back window under a large tree that cast a permanent and frightening shade.

Salvador: *Is anyone coming?*

Kapre: *No, no one, except reinforcements.*

With doubtful might, he uprooted a sapling from the ground and offered it to his protector as a toothpick. Salvador was hiding in the South, and was delighted to hear that there were reinforcements on their way from Pampanga.

That morning of March 23, 1901, the Macabebes arrived at a shore near Palanan, which was still recovering from the big celebration of Salvador's thirty-second birthday, the day before.

Salvador: *The little village was in gala dress. Arches had been erected, and there were other decorations provided despite limited resources. A number of people had made the fifty-mile journey from Casiguran to congratulate me on the occasion, and we celebrated the day with horse races, dancing, serenades, and amateur theatrics. The approach of reinforcements furnished an added incentive to the festivity of the day.*

The Macabebes and their prisoners journeyed inland and, after several days, they ran out of supplies. When they got close enough to Salvador's camp they asked for supplies, because they couldn't go on without them. According to the memoirs of the Spanish intelligence agent Lieutenant Ejercito, upon entering the town the Macabebes were like children who wanted to laugh but were trying not to spoil the joke.

Ejercito, using a forged letter, entered Salvador's office posing as the reinforcements.

Good to see you friend, you're in good shape. Are you happy with the men General Lacuna has sent?

This was followed by a fifteen-minute conversation about tides and the fruits in season. Salvador kept looking away from the velvet curtains, and then upon realising that Ejercito may at some point turn his head and note the violet horror too, Salvador promptly tied the curtains up into a ponytail.

Salvador: *These men are hungry. Please give them some more food!*

And then suddenly the Spanish lieutenant stood up and motioned towards the window and yelled, *Now, Macabebes! Bes-bes-bes.*

Salvador: *What? I didn't hear what you said. Naumaa...*

Gun-fire! Gun-fire! Gun-fire, gun-fire, gun-fire!
Pukhawwww. Pukhawww.

Salvador thought – a celebratory toast! Are they firing
in the air? Were his guards attacking his guests?

*Cease-fire! Cease-fire! Cease-fire, cease-fire, cease-fire!
This is ridiculous, totally a mistake, hold your fire, cook
your rice, what is going on?!*

Macabebes: *Long live the Macabebes! Bes-bes-bes.*

Tigidig, tigidig, digidig.

He looked out of the window and realised that his men
were being shot at, and that those attacking them were the
legendary Macabebes, dressed in guerrilla uniforms. They
let their hair roll down from beneath their caps, *wish, wish.*
He couldn't tell whether he was more frightened by the hair
or the rifles. He hid behind the velvet curtain.

*I seized a revolver, intending to defend myself, but Dr
Barcelona threw his arms at me, crying out: 'Don't sacrifice
yourself. Your country needs you.'*

Thus, I was prevented from carrying out my intention.

They pulled him out from behind the curtains and shot at
him. A bullet bounced on the velvet curtain, and Salvador
realised that it was solid and not liquid. It was magic. They
shot again, and the bullets went beneath his armpits.
Another brushed through his hair.

The Macabebes chased him around the room.

*Okay, that's enough. I am Frederick Funston of the US Army.
You are now a prisoner of war.*

Announcer: *It isn't known whether Salvador's charm
resisted the bullets and that was how he came to be captured
alive. Of his guards, only one man was killed – perhaps
he forgot to wear his bulletproof vest – and two were
wounded.*

Later, Paris, a city irrelevant to the situation, received a
cablegram that said: According to precise information, the
man captured is not Diego Salvador, but Baldomero Salvador,
chief of the general staff, and Diego's cousin. This information
was incorrect.

Salvador: *A little later I was presented to General MacArthur
as a prisoner of war. Such was my return after an absence
of four years.*

Salvador died in 1961, and pictures of him are imprinted on
billions of five peso coins. Funston and Salvador's children
would shake hands in the nineteen-twenties, when both were
students at Westpoint.

≈

I was sitting next to a woman in the lobby of the Turagsoy
Hotel. It had only been opened two years, but the hotel
was passably art deco, with a quadratura ceiling that depicted
seven moons and an extremely cloudy sky. The walls were
stained, as if it had been raining from the artificial representation
above them. The lounge, disconnected from the hotel's

architecture, was inspired by an Irish pub. It smelled
of cockroaches and old cabinets. On each table there was
a rose which the lighting made look both black and red.
The hallways out of the lobby were hung with damaged
mirrors held together with duct tape.

There was a man sleeping on the couch beside me, hugging
his radio.

DJ 1: *I tell you, the previous administration may have been
intelligent but they didn't care for anyone but themselves.
If only I didn't fear the Lord – I would do so many
unimaginably evil acts I can't even tell you – they would
feel the punishment of the Lord.*

DJ 2: *The Lord said do not blame others. Fanatical supporters
of the previous administration need to learn that. They are
stubborn, stubborn people. We must all pray for our Lord
Mayor Cowboy and the president of our country.*

DJ 1: *Yes, caller...*

Caller: *You know, what if the entire country becomes full
of drug lords – not the ones who were killed in the drug war
but those who orchestrated it so that they could kill off the
competition. And then what. And then when Federalism is
enacted, the drug lords will take over each region. And then
what. And then they'll take over the free ports of each region
which used to be the stronghold of the largest non-Catholic
denomination. And then what. And then the grandson of
the largest church group will come out of his shell and then
act like a man of the people and proclaim himself a pope.
And then what. And then he will go from town to town
and proclaim the good word and incite everyone to fight*

with him against the oppressive drug lords, with the promise of gold and Chinese imports. And then what. And then it would be a battle between the…

DJ 2: *Wow. Sorry we got cut off there. Ah – uh, now here's Shirley Bassey, ah uh.*

DJ 1: *That would be a bestselling book, no! Or a blockbuster Viva Films movie…*

DJ 2: *Shirley Bassey, 'This Is My Life'.*

The coffee tasted like it was mixed with corn flavouring, like the sweet corn powder-coated French fries that they sell in the office canteen. But this brew was entirely made out of burnt corn husks and contained no caffeine.

Will this give me palpitations?

It doesn't have caffeine.

She poured me another cup. The grounds had been steeped for a few minutes in boiling water and then trained, the burnt corn husks giving the drink a roasted taste. The charcoal in it promised to ease the gut, a charm for stomachs troubled by flatulence, anxiety, and frequent food poisoning.

I mean, you can order regular coffee, if you like?

This substitute was used during the war when there was no coffee available, or at least not at a price most could afford. It remained available because people had got used to the taste and coffee was still too expensive.

Belen once told me rice coffee was used as a contraceptive. She made her eyes very big and mimicked a mother scolding a daughter in a slow angry voice, *Burn that rice and boil it for a long, long time...* Superstition had it that menstruation came right back.

Caller: *So, I went to bed early, and didn't celebrate New Year. I spent the first day of the year cleaning up fireworks floating on the water. They were everywhere. I just wanted to help clean up. My nephew and I were just picking debris out of the ocean. I swam out a bit, until I was neck-deep in the water, and reached out for something that looked like cardboard. Grabbed it. It was mushy. It turned out to be shit.*

Beside me was a woman whose name I've forgotten. We'd once been friends. She had her view toward the lounge singer who was crooning 'Take My Breath Away'. Her head resembled the movements of a pigeon.

She said, *Good to see you, good to see you... Last night as I was showering I saw that there were black spots on the wall next to the glass. Large moles. I don't know where they came from – maybe the ceiling or something. I then took a tissue and really tried to scratch them out with the edge of my fingernail but I couldn't get rid of them. They were stubborn. I then decided to just go to sleep. When I woke up this morning the spots were completely gone!*

Maybe they had evaporated?

My friend was leaning on a fake pebble wall with an aquarium embedded in it. The wall looked like it was sweating ochre. As we chatted, we had to keep our feet up because a distraught young waiter with a floral waistcoat was screaming as he tried to kill a mouse with a plastic fly swatter. As he bopped his weak weapon furiously on the ground, the creature scrambled for safety beneath our chairs. The singer looked our way as she sang 'Nothing's Gonna Change My Love for You'. My friend seemed not to notice.

The spots couldn't have disappeared. The shower was so hot and I spent so long scratching away. I swear I left them still on the wall. Here, I have a photo of just what they looked like. I don't understand how they could just disappear! I couldn't get the stain out! I want to understand how it happened!

Maybe you scratched them away without realising it.

I had my phone flashlight on. You can do that with your phone, right? No, I remember leaving it and giving up. I remember seeing the marks still there.

She had a soft voice but emphasised her esses, and everything else was a whisper. In my mind, I saw her as a snake.

That's strange.

Yes, very strange, which was why I really needed to tell someone what happened. I was in Room 514. True story. They just disappeared. By the way, it was hard to sleep because of the sound of the drainage coming from other rooms when people showered! Can you tell her to sing 'Ocean Deep'?

≈

Rodrigo is in a gay nightclub with two elderly folk. One wears a gold turban and an electric blue robe – all silk.

Wang Chung's 'Everybody Have Fun Tonight' is playing.

Friend 1: *Hey, did you know your dad and I are old pals?*

Rodrigo: *Oh?*

Friend 2: *Your dad is our brother in the confederation of transvestite crime fighters. But we don't see him so often because we're abroad a lot, inhabiting all sorts of worlds. Your dad just suddenly disappeared one day. We've just come back from Italy.*

Rodrigo: *You must be making a mistake. Are you being true-blue?*

Friend 2: *No doubt about it. Wanna bet?*

Friend 1: *Put a mask on him. Change his blood and body. And intestines. I'd recognise him anywhere.*

Rodrigo: *Nah. My father is Pacifico Mana-lash-tash...*

Friend 1: *Correct! Pacifico Manalastas and Facifica Falayfay are the same person.*

Everybody, everyone... Everybody Wang Chung tonight...

Rodrigo imagines an empty dance floor with a pink fairy in the middle. The fairy is encased in a plastic curtain. The translucent covering is removed, revealing Facifica Falayfay wearing a blonde wig and a big scarf made of tulle.

In a later scene, Pacifico Manalastas himself shows up at the club as Facifica. She enters the club wearing a black-and-white striped dress and sits quietly observing the scene, waiting to bust some drug dealers. She pulls her blue sunglasses down her nose to take a good look. Everybody's dancing to Finzi Kontini's 'O La La'. Cut to a room where a briefcase is opened and a drug deal is being made. *Maybe the solution's every time I hit the floor. How can I refuse temptation knockin' at my door?* Facifica's confederates and son are exhausted from dancing and sit next to her table. She notices her son and faces away toward the electric blue wall. Friend 1 recognises her. She stands in front of the undercover detective, bends forward, and yells *Facificaaaa!* She bops Friend 1 on her bald forehead. Her son spits out his drink.

Facifica: *That's not me!*

Friend 1: *You haven't changed. I'm with your child, Rhoda!*

Rhoda stands in front of her.

Rhoda / Rodrigo: *Hypocrite! Liar! You beat me up because you're ashamed that I'm gay. Turns out, you're gay too! You kicked me out of the house! You took away my right to call you Daddy. Well, I take back your right to call me your son!*

Facifica: *Shh. Please don't…*

Rodrigo: *I'm going to out you – Pacifico Manalastaaaaas! Pwe!*

The thugs turn around. Facifica pulls a gun from her red purse and shoots.

≈

About a kilometre away from the red river, a family was getting
ready to share a butterfly-style fried knife fish for dinner.

The teenage son was trying to do the sitting-and-rising test
that he had recently learned in physical education but he wasn't
the athletic sort. His parents were yelling at each other. The
grandfather had one hand on the leg of a heavy table because
his fingers hurt when held at other angles, while the other
held his paper.

Five men entered the small hut. The grandfather looked up
at the mother and announced, *Your guests are here.*

What guests?

The men quickly tied the family up with their hands behind
their backs. They were left seated on the ground. The robbers
ransacked the modest home.

It occurred to the grandfather that someone was missing.
Where is Nina?

As the men knocked down her father, Nina had run out the
house and into the village where she yelled for help but her
betrothed and his friends were blind drunk on gin. *Think
about the marriage! Fool!* Nina picked up a bolo knife
and held it in two hands and judged from the weight that
it thwacked perfectly.

There's no money here.

There's no money here, what are you talking about...

Hiyunk!

The mother was pistol-whipped in her face and the clasp
of her Holy Trinity necklace broke.

Meanwhile, Nina raised the bolo knife with both hands
above her head and ran back home. She was known in
the town for running 100m in a record of 13 seconds,
and given that it was about 200m to get back home,
it took approximately 26 seconds.

The leader of the gang had decided to have a bite of the
hot butterflied fish, and as he formed his hand into a pincer,
Nina crept up behind him and sliced off his shoulder from
behind, bringing his heart out with it. His head fell forward
into the wok of still-hot oil. In a panic, the men fired their
guns at her, hitting windows, doorframes, bitter gourd,
the Pope John Paul calendar, and the fillet of fish. They
had not practiced firing before and didn't expect to use
their guns. Their failing to sink a bullet in her made Nina,
for that moment, invincible. The boys ran as she chased
them, promising to hack them to pieces if she caught
them up.

Many town locals attended the funeral procession for
the half-body man whose dismembered torso had been
duct-taped and promptly ejected from the ossuary. Women
were crying because he was a former teacher, who'd also run
a gambling den in the town library that was bereft of books
but overflowed with debts. His eyes behind shades, Cowboy
led the procession, riding his motorcycle at a crawl, as a
public-address system played the song 'While There Is Life'.
The two fifteen-year-olds, heads down, but out of the jail
cells and absolved, but still in handcuffs for reasons we

don't know, were lagging at the back of the procession, crying with their lower lips turned out.

An inter-city bus driver was trying to make his journey from one town to another on the national highway, a journey that on big quota days needed a lot of speed, was singing Mariah Carey's 'Butterfly' as he swung carelessly around the corner. *Spread your wings and prepare to fly, for you have bee-come a butterfly… O-o-o-O fly determinedly into the sun…* He miscalculated the trajectory and hit the two teenagers, necessitating another funeral procession.

Once Bayot came to visit and bought a jar of Belen's tears. He told us about the latest research at the University of San Pablo. He had learned that if hirsutism is genetic we were direct descendants of Macabebe Marie. We were river people. He asked if we'd like it if he arranged for her bust to be erected on a seven-foot column of green stone. It would be made from the same Italian marble that had been used in the walls of the old radio station. He went on. *The plaque could say: 'Macabebe Marie was born to be a warrior. She was beautiful and she was hirsute, she was often mistaken for a boy, which she used to her own advantage. She was an exceptional mercenary. Like any Macabebe, she wasn't really a gun for hire, or particularly conspiratorial, she believed that her only real enemy was Tagalog, although the Macabebes had joined forces with their tribal nemesis to free themselves from the grasp of the Spaniards who had oppressed them for three hundred years. And in this revolution, as the nation slowly formed, the pushing together of the land made it feel as if these ancient enmities were reaching a necessary close. Not yet, they said, not yet.'* The mayor folded the paper he'd been reading from, and used it to wipe away a tear.

While thousands of Macabebes sided with Spain against
the insurrection, some fought alongside the Katipuneros
against the Castilians. Macabebe Marie, and her husband,
sank swords into the chest of Spain – metaphorically, because
the islands were more like a forefinger and of little interest
to the weakening mother power and soon sold for a paltry
sum to the USA in the Treaty of Paris. Marie's husband
died leading troops in battle and so, in her grief, she took
his sword and uniform and became a captain, commanding
the army of Baliwag.

Macabebe Marie's favourite tactic was ambush. She was
under the personal command of Diego Salvador, who had
announced that those who were wounded in battle would
receive the sum of 50 pesos. Macabebe Marie was wounded
three times. She demanded the sum of 150 pesos for the
three incidents. It is said that Salvador did not pay her.

Short-changed and angered by this cheap treatment, she
defected to the Americans and revealed everything she knew
about Salvador's plans to the colonial power. She became
a spy, and could draw confessions out of anyone whether
she was dressed as a soldier, a beggar, a man, or a woman.

Not much else is known about her. It is said that General
Funston who commanded the Macabebes for the Americans
was frustrated by all the ladrones, or bandits, who extorted
tribute from the people. Funston was determined to get rid
of them, but whenever he sent his men out to catch them,
they returned and said they had found no bandits, just some
'friendly natives'. So Macabebe Marie took two sergeants
out with her shortly before nightfall and took shelter in an
unprotected house. She was cooking dinner outside while
her two Americans soldiers remained inside. Before long,

five ladrones came in with their bolo knives. Macabebe Marie rushed into the house, shot two dead and captured the other three.

Is this true? I asked Bayot.

You have hair on your cheeks, don't you?!

Macabebe Marie was not hirsute.

The mayor, alias Cowboy, named for his red cowboy hat made from a weave that appeared to warp, was rumoured to have strangled his second son, alias Bayot, last week and accidentally killed him in the foyer after a heated argument. Bayot, thirty-two, a meek reformist, had been locked up in the house for twenty days because of his left-wing position and possession of copies of work from the world's leading radical thinkers – though none of the titles had been read, because his entire book collection was still shrink-wrapped in plastic, except for Rhonda Byrne's *The Secret*. He will be remembered for wanting to convert the big gambling den on the edge of the town into the library it had been intended to be by the national government, and for wanting to create a cryptozoological society in his free time.

The Bayot situation was a problem as big as the time a man named Rudy and his mistress visited the town on a motorcycle and stayed in the 'I Love You' Condotel. Their talking became arguing – *fondling, at the beginning of the street*, said one witness, and *screaming, at the end* said another. The lovers had not seen the curve in the road. A man driving a large provincial bus, listening to Mariah Carey's 'Butterfly', also did not see the curve. Nothing could prevent Rudy from being hit, then flying and impaling himself on the spike of a tall fence.

Rudy was Cowboy's first-born son, a decorated colonel who'd escaped jail for shooting a piano-playing bartender. The bus driver, Mark, stopped the music and stepped out of the bus. *No more, no more, this is not what I was meant to do in life.* He assumed the identity of a British man and established a dive bar with the emblem of a pale mermaid or pez mulier. He called the bar 'Butterfly'.

It is not possible to explain Cowboy's popularity. His father, the previous mayor, had killed nearly every grown son in Cowboy's generation, but either people had forgotten or they simply enjoyed the idea of continuity. Cowboy, who was unchallenged as mayor for twenty years – except for a few attempts on his life, all of which he'd swiftly avenged by killing the perpetrators – owed at least some of his popularity to an actor also known as Cowboy, a large bullish figure who also sported a thin moustache. The action star played Cowboy the mayor in a biopic, who killed thousands of people during an all-out war against hunger.

The entire scene is like Michelangelo's *Battle of the Centaurs*, or at least its reproduction in a coffee table book. It appears as though humans are trying to fight their way out of being cast permanently into the relief, and so they're just pushing other people into the marble, a complete slosh of bodies all mushed together. It becomes hard to determine where the Lapiths were and where the Centaurs stood. It just looks like a bunch of men brawling.

Cowboy's family owned the land by way of generations of mayoralties and also ran the largest restaurant in the

province, Noble Court (Open 24 Hours), located on
a two-hectare plot where the locals spent their birthdays
and graduations. With Cowboy in jail, Bayot celebrated
his birthday every week. The third-generation mayor, alias
Bayot, a former set designer, believed that people should
be taught how to enjoy life, and it was his right, destiny,
privilege, honour, and duty to share what he knew. Although
it was compulsory for adults to attend, they were free to
continue believing in Feng Shui and witches and centaurs.
By attending his birthday, Bayot simply wanted us to learn
how to discuss important events, figures, and the political
issues of the day. *It is recommended that you speak with
a British accent to calm the nerves*, he said.

Caterers would set up tall tables but no chairs. Teenage
volunteers wore white shirts and black bow ties and
distributed white and red wine. We were treated to a
long buffet of tuna and salmon sushi with wasabi, sculpted
in the shape of a fish; red hotdogs, alkaline water, Four
Seasons Iced Tea, Long Island Iced Tea, Californian maki
rolls, chicken lollipop, beef stroganoff, ludong, the President's
fish; Food for the Gods, arroz a la Cubana, baked Alaska,
shawarma, peach melba, galantina, macaroons, Campbell's
mushroom soup, red wine jus, pot-au-feu, tuna pie, Java
rice, lumpiang Shanghai, mango Samurai Crepe, calamares,
casserole, coleslaw, chocolate crinkles, creamy carbonara,
corn dog, Karo corn syrup, club sandwich, chocolate
fountain, curly parsley, crab meat Dewey, chicken a la
Kiev, chicken a la king, pata-tim, galbi chim, baby back
ribs, tuna Niçoise, Thousand Island dressing, sizzling
mushrooms, sizzling T-bone steak, Salisbury steak,
rum cake, pound cake, Bundt cake, butter cake, mocha
cake, angel's food cake, devil's food cake, Black Forest
cake, bochi, maraschino, cheese pimiento, mango sago,

fettuccine Alfredo, osso buco, taco salad, macaroni salad, fruit salad, gambas, aspic, sans rival, banana split, hash brown, Hungarian sausage, ham with pineapple glaze, spaghetti Bolognese, Pina Colada, Kamikaze, Sex on the Beach, Blow Job, and Weng Weng.

Out-of-town visitors were permitted to watch and take pictures of the extravagance, with their SLRs slung over their sunburned napes. Many were offended, and wrote conscientious think pieces starting with *'One must lament that the large styrofoam float was...'*

A recent mayoral candidate (the first challenger) had tried to make it part of his platform to rid us of this extravaganza, but he was always at the events standing alone beside the hired band and touching his face. Some, like Pilita, were incensed at having to attend such a flagrant set-up, but it was not entirely unwelcome for others, like Ma, who preferred it to cable television.

Cowboy returned after a long and mysterious absence. *Fucking son of a whore.* He turned up to the party as dance instructors were on stage showing people how to dance to DeBarge's 'Rhythm of the Night'. Cowboy lifted his gun high and shot through the corrugated roof twice, so that the party noticed that it had been raining. The crowd ran everywhere because there was no clear exit. Cowboy stepped away from the leak he had made in the roof, shot the dance instructors, and pulled Bayot by the ear. Whoever attended the parties, Cowboy said, would be thrown to the crocodiles.

Bayot was giving away free condoms. Cowboy threw him out of office and reinstalled himself as mayor.

≈

In the 1941 film adaptation of *Ibong Adarna*, three princes
stood by a well. The youngest, Principe Juan, tied some
vines together and used them to climb down the well.
After some time, the second prince, worried that he might
need help, followed him. The eldest and least trustworthy
stayed behind. The first prince had discovered a subterranean
kingdom where he'd caught sight of a beautiful cave-dwelling
princess named Leonora. He assumed that she needed to
be saved from the giant with the club, and helped her escape
by battling him. The giant was too clumsy to be a proper
opponent and was easy game. The prince threw a rock
at his head, which concussed the giant, and then followed
up by throwing a large spade that pierced his neck.
It was the size of a toothpick for the monster but he
died immediately.

Come with me, demanded the prince.

Where?

Above ground.

But what am I going to do there?

Let's get married.

They rushed back to the well, where they met the second
prince coming down the rope. They sent Princess Leonora
up first. It was a very deep well.

Well! What are you looking at! Pull! she commanded the
eldest prince Pedro when she got to the top of the well.

You fell from heaven, said Principe Pedro.

Fell from heaven? I came from underground!

Principe Pedro cut the rope and left with the princess.

When night fell, a big voice from above told the gallant Principe Juan and his elder brother Diego that there were two beautiful princesses who lived in the Reino de los Cristales.

But are they prettier than Princesa Leonora?

Nobody can beat how beautiful and intelligent the two princesses are. The voice turned out to be a giant eagle, the size of a helicopter, and they clung on to its legs. The bird dropped them on the ground.

They found the two girls swimming naked in their private pool. The two men used a stick to pull away their clothes which were on the other side of a fence. When the princesses had finished their swim, they looked for their underwear. The brothers returned it piece by piece from outside the enclosure.

Are you mad at us? Principe Juan asked.

No, we liked it, of course, replied one of the princesses. *Guards!*

The guards surrounded them.

It is normal for somebody in love to find any way to introduce himself to the object of his desire, Principe Juan explained.

If you want to introduce yourselves, then do so to our father,
said Princess Maria. *Guards!*

They brought the two princes to the palace to meet their
father, who was the king and a sorcerer.

What were you doing by my daughters' bathing area?
What are you doing in my kingdom?, the king demanded.
The production crew had glued white cotton around
his cheeks and made two big balls on his chin.

We are here to serve you and do as you command, said
Principe Diego.

As I command? The king and his right-hand man laughed.

Principe Juan, do you see that mountain over there?
Move the damn thing and have it right outside my window
tomorrow morning. If you fail, I will chop your head off.

The prince hid his head in Princess Maria's breasts and
feared the morning. She realised that she was in love with
the prince too.

I told you not to worry. I can do it. Princess Maria reached
out of the window and used magic to drag the mountain
a short distance from the palace. The camera zoomed
in on the mountain to make it appear as though it was
coming closer.

The following day the king challenged the young man again.

Principe Juan, do you see that mountain that you have
brought to my window?

Yes.

Flatten it. Here's a bag of wheat. Plant it and make me bread for breakfast. And if you fail, I will bury you alive.

But that's impossible! he cried. *And if I do it?*

Then I'll give you anything you want.

Later, by her bedroom window, Princess Maria was about to throw the bag of wheat at the mountain. *Wait, no*, said the prince, unassured of the princess's feelings. *I'd rather be buried alive than live without being loved by you.*

The princess walked over to the middle of the room, where there was a column that looked like a transparent shower curtain because the stage set was vaguely Moorish. They sang a duet together.

Oh no! They realised they'd spent a long time singing. *We haven't levelled the mountain yet.*

The princess went to the window and clapped. With each clap, the mountain grew smaller and smaller. This scene is realised with a wonderfully bleak stop-motion of a mountain's silhouette at dusk. There is an invisible pounding, left, right, left, right, until the mountain is no more.

The wheat! Give me the wheat!

The princess threw it at the mountain and, in seconds, the straws became a wheat field.

Get out of here! The king said to the prince, upon receiving the bread that he'd ordered.

The princes stole two horses from the stable and the princesses came to meet them. Princesa Isabel and Principe Diego got a head start while the remaining two lagged behind. When the king found out, he gathered his men, and rode out after them.

What do we do? They'll catch up to us! yelled the helpless Principe Juan.

Don't worry! Princess Maria pulled soap from her bag and threw it behind them. *I'll turn this mountain into soap!*

Yikes, said the king's right hand, when they got close. *That mountain is slippery!*

But the king somehow overcame the soap mountain.

Oh no, they're still catching up with us! yelled a prince.

Well. Only a big body of water can truly separate us! The princess pulled out a rectangular crystal, that looked like a small block of clear water, from her clothes. She blessed it and threw it behind her, and it became a sea.

Damn my own daughter! I cast a curse to make Principe Juan forget about the princess completely!

≈

The local authority erected a large bust of Cowboy high up a mountain. It was inspired by Mount Rushmore. The hat proved difficult to make and it took months to construct the mould. Three months after it was unveiled, unknown persons blew it up. The bust wasn't carved out of the mountain after all. *It's not pure stone, it's concrete!* The explosion revealed a hollow head with steel matting for veins. Many believed the dynamite was laid not in protest but because there were rumours that Yamashita's treasure was kept inside. Others blamed the communists. When Cowboy visited his ruined likeness, he buried his real head in his hands.

I heard an explosion, said Pilita. *Did the volcano – oop!*

I was standing on one of the round fold-out banquet tables in the Triad Coffee Shop, because I believed that at a high altitude I was closer to heaven. I was watching a man in the distance shooting into the air, as if alone in a spaghetti western. The cafe overlooked the bust, and before the explosion, had been a popular tourist destination promoted by the mayor himself.

The cafe boasted a laminated menu of 3-in-1 coffees, and the waitresses carried the big jelly ices in fat sundae glasses, which looked like plump white ducklings, on their trays.

The staff turned on the television and I focused my attention on the faded screen. In the film, a group of old ladies, wearing pearl necklaces and thick blouses, were sitting down to have lunch.

Mrs Sophie T Curtis: *Three beers for my cohorts and a double Old Fashioned for me, I'm driving.*

Trudy: *It wouldn't be Tuesday if you didn't come in here Mrs Curtis. Guess what the special is for today.*

Mrs Curtis: *Salmon aspic?*

Trudy: *Tomato surprise.*

Mrs. Gibson: *Yeccch.*

Trudy: *Two coffees and two hot teas?*

Sylvia Sidney starred as Mrs Gibson in *Do Not Fold, Spindle, or Mutilate*, a film about four old women who find themselves in trouble when they create a fake lonely heart profile and send it off to a computer dating agency to catfish men for fun.

Over lunch, they created a persona named Rebecca Mead and answered a questionnaire for her.

Mrs. Gibson: *Are we really going to send it in?*

Mrs. Curtis: *Of course. How would we get any answers if we didn't? Here are some of the questions…*

Mrs. Saunders: *This is so exciting!*

Mrs. Curtis: *'Do you believe in intimate contact before marriage?' The answers are 'yes', 'no', and 'depends on the circumstances'. I think 'depends on the circumstances'.*

Mrs. Saunders: *You don't!*

Mrs. Curtis: *Well not me personally, dear. The girl we're making up that's going to join this silly thing does.*

Mrs. Saunders: *'Depending on the circumstances' means the same as 'yes', Sophie T!*

Mrs. Curtis: *'Is it important to you that your date shares your attitudes about sex?' Answers: yes, no, moderately. In deference to you, Shelby we'll tick moderately.*

Mrs. Gibson: *Are all the questions that intimate?*

Mrs. Curtis: *Oh, of course not, I'm just picking out the good ones for now.*

Mrs. Saunders: *What's the name of the girl that's supposedly doing this thing?*

Mrs. Curtis: *Rebecca Mead. There isn't a single, solitary Rebecca Mead in Pasadena – or in any of the surrounding towns.*

Mrs. Tyson: *Is that what you were doing with those phone books, Sophie?*

Mrs. Curtis: *Well, we couldn't very well use the name of a real person. And Aunt Becky would be so happy if she knew we were thinking of her!*

Mrs. Saunders: *This is much more fun than when we registered for the draft! What's next Sophie T?*

Mrs. Curtis: *They want to know her age.*

Mrs. Gibson: *Oh, ah, twenty-three is a nice age!*

Mrs. Curtis: *Twenty-three. Just old enough, but not too old.*

Mrs. Tyson: *'Just old enough but not too old' for what, Sophie T?*

Mrs. Curtis: *I'm too old to remember.*

The bored old ladies paid little attention to the consequences of the whole set-up, preferring their daytime drinking, and failed to cancel the profile, which stayed on the computer until a match was made.

A writer named Malcolm Weston insisted upon meeting Rebecca after murdering a hooker he'd met at a bar, who he'd mistakenly assumed was the non-existent Mead.

Mal went to the Curtis house looking for the 'real' Rebecca Mead.

Mrs. Curtis: *Young man, this will come as a shock,*
I'm certain – but there is no Rebecca Mead…

Mal Weston: *Now don't give me any of that garbage!*

Mrs Curtis: *There never was a Rebecca Mead, not lately,*
anyhow.

Mrs. Tyson: *Rebecca Mead is our aunt and she went*
to her reward years and years ago.

Mrs. Curtis: *So, there's no need for you to be here at all!*

Mrs. Saunders: *Sophie T!*

Mrs. Curtis: *And you're frightening Shelby – Mrs. Saunders.*

I turned away from the movie because I couldn't breathe. Phlegm pooled in my throat. I needed to leave, and struggled to stand up. A waiter holding a cast-iron plate was rushing

to set it down. The waiter yelled, *Sizzling plate, careful it's hot!*
Half my body swung to dodge him, but we both moved in the
same direction.

Ouch!

Sir, I told you it was hot!

I sat down to recover. Oil had spattered across my shirt in
tamarind-shaped patterns. The pain from my sciatic nerve ran
along my thigh down to my foot. The pain was just below the
ankle, at the point that, in statues of the crucifixion, Jesus is
shown to have had a nail driven through his flesh. Sceptics say
these nails couldn't have supported a man's weight, forgetting
that Christ isn't a man, he is the Son of God. The table seemed
to rise up and hit my elbows. I got up to leave. The waitress
handed me a bill for 666 pesos. The man beside the table had
the perfume of an overbearing aunt. He was lecturing the
waitress about our surroundings.

*That's the sound of a bird that looks like a calabria, it's the size
of a thumb and it is blue. It's so loud it sings twenty-four hours.*

*That's the sound of the kingfisher. He's got all of the goldfish,
there's nothing left in the pond. Well, now he can eat the toads.
He should eat the toads.*

≈

Hundreds of birds slamming against our window did not
wake Pilita.

She lay flat on her back. She reminded me of a dead tokay
gecko. Her arms were outstretched and her legs were spread

open. Her chin appeared to point north. The pores along
her upper lip were, like a boiled chicken, yellow, wrinkly
and bristly to the finger. I touched her arm hair and it felt like
old-fashion silk organza. She saw things because she always
slept with her eyes partially open. Her eyes were so big there
was not enough skin to wrap around them. She was dead now.

She had been a vegetable for a while; an old patola, a hairy
gourd. She ate so many Hershey's Kisses that her brain bled and
she had a stroke. I imagined her suffering through an eternal
migraine. But what if she had lost the will to die and preferred
to live? I said, *Pilita, do you want to live?*, and she said nothing.
So, I let her be until she opened her eyes as if awake, and
breathed her last and the final gust travelled out her buttocks.
The velocity of her death rattle shook the church bells.

Sometimes the love we have for people is strained by too
many words, as if we need to carry out a long conversation
to prove closeness. I asked her yesterday, *Did the Xerox
boy's wife give birth yet?*

What's Xerox?

I shrugged impatiently. It was our last conversation.

I thought I saw Pilita's cheek muscles contract. I thought
of what I'd been told by Father Low about Luigi Galvani
making the legs of dead frogs kick by passing an electric
current through their cadavers. And that their muscles
would twitch if salt was sprinkled over them. I thought
about pouring salt over Pilita. I felt frightened.

I told you about Belen, Pilita said, her subtle body watching
over her prone flesh. *Over my dead body.*

The morning after Pilita passed on was identical to the day she died. I was woken by shouting on the street. An MC took to the microphone; his tiredness and the extra heat made his excitement sound like anger. He had been selling Suzuki motorcycles since the crack of dawn. A poster of Cowboy that I could see from my window had been bleached by the sun and only the blue ink remained. I splashed water over my face and carried Pilita's body to the ossuary.

I'd lost my grandmother and I'd lost my home. I went to stay at the Turagsoy Condotel. The rooms were priced for North Americans and Koreans. Most locals couldn't afford them. Everybody knows that if you are a solo traveller and take a room with two single beds, a spirit will sleep next to you. Pale figures in long white gowns, taking their soft room slippers off and lying down, watching you across the bed. It's worse if you have a queen bed.

There were no single rooms left. *But I remember you*, the owner of the condotel remarked. *You sold that magic fish that cleaned out my mother-in-law's kidneys. You killed her!* He laughed. *Ah, you can come stay for free – but you get a big room since it's all we have left.*

I turned around to face the empty squat oval lobby, and recommended that the hotel spirits choose a different room to sleep in that evening. *Not room 435!* I pointed at the unremarkable family with matching bowl cuts and dive fins when they were not looking. I raised both hands up for attention. *I just need some peace*, I yelled.

The sound of the crickets by a large dark fountain in front of the hotel and the on-off of the nocturnal tikling felt like being back home. At an easy distance, an old man was setting

down bamboo traps for mudskippers at midnight. It was
a warm night, and the fan turned left and right, as if it were
saying, *No – I am very disappointed in this adventure that*
you are currently undertaking – No – I am very disappointed,
left, right, left, right, and the wind eventually started to
irritate my arm hairs. I saw shadows in the windows that
appeared like flying salamanders, but they could have easily
been bats. Or it could have been the tokay gecko. A large
American GI Jerry that I once met called them 'Tucker'.
With the fan on level three, the highest power level, it made
the journey very difficult for the mosquitos, hard for them
to needle into my thighs. I had to withstand the irritation
because I was too exhausted to clap or clasp at them with
my hand. Even so, I did, and mosquito reinforcements just
kept coming out of the stagnant fountain. Motorcycle engines
popped and puttered by, carrying yodelling drunks home.
It all made sleep impossible.

I cleaned my face using a small bar of soap. It was coarse,
as if it was made of compacted grease and chalk. I was afraid
to close my eyes as I soaped my eyelids in case I opened them
and discovered something horrific had happened. That said,
I was afraid to touch stair rails and door handles, in case
they'd recently been used by someone whose hand had
rubbed a dog's face and got its rheum on it. And, in turn,
if I rubbed the morning glory into my eyes and looked
in the mirror, I'd see my ancestors. Or are they just strangers?
I want to be alone in the bathroom but I know someone
else is there. I always worry something is staring at me while
I poo, so I look around the entire bathroom trying to lock
eyes everywhere hoping to intimidate them.

When I need time to think I sit on the toilet with my pants
down, armed with a plastic mosquito racket set to high

voltage. I feel wonderful every time I manage to zap one
of the bloodsuckers with an electric shock. Mosquitoes
have given my legs a consistent look, leaving them dotted
with round scars as if I played outside. The boys on my
street would climb trees but not me. They always tried
to peek into my window, from which I was always was
looking at them. Once one of them fell and hit his shoulder
on an old root. I wanted to laugh but tried to suppress
it because I was afraid I would fall too. I showed no emotion
as I stared out the window. They already thought I was
a witch.

I left the light on as a precaution.

As I closed my eyes, I remembered being on Turagsoy
beach for the first time. Ma never took us. We had lived
here all our lives but didn't go there because Ma thought
I'd be picked on and there were dangerously high amounts
of E. coli in the water. She told me I was too hairy to wear
a bikini. She warned me that the water would burn my
flesh off. My schoolmates could not believe that I thought
that would happen. They stripped me down to my scrubs.
One of them pushed me to the water where I expected
to die, and as I fell I prayed to the Lord Almighty. When
I emerged I was a different person. I drank the water
that gave me life. Later I vomited in the bathroom, and
I remember that our hennas were still wet so we were
unable to sleep on the bed or else we would have to pay
for staining the linen. Anyway, the old man said, *Why
don't you go home because your house is only ten minutes
away?* He didn't want our money and would have charged
foreigners a lot more than a local like me. But the place was
nearly empty, as were our pockets, and he later chased us
out with a broomstick.

I was in high school when I returned to the beach. I had two glasses of Cali Shandy and felt that the world was spinning, so I had to sit by a rock. I watched a woman emerge from the dance area of the bar. She squatted down and took a shit on the beach. She faced the horizon as her excrement left her body. There were about a hundred people five feet away from her, just watching. And when she'd finished, she stood up and returned to the bar where she shook her body to pop beats.

I was afraid of the power of my own body. But the only person who took any interest in me was an extra-large sex tourist with red eye bags and a paper hat over his head, dancing and spinning around.

He pointed his finger right at me. I ran and hid in the darkness of the water.

I dozed for ten minutes but malicious laughter broke my sleep. From the darkness outside, I thought I had a waterfront view, but when I drew back the maroon curtains I found myself looking at a concrete wall onto which a beach scene had been painted. There was a warm white bulb in the centre of the mural's sun. Beneath my window and that wall there were a few hens imprisoned inside upside-down copper mesh laundry hampers.

It looked to me as if dawn was breaking above two large trees. The emerging sun was a red orange disc that glowed like cigarette lighters in old cars.

I heard three or four heavy stomps. I could smell the smoke from a cigar. This made me think of Jerry's breath. I wanted to crawl underneath the bed but it was too low for my buttocks to fit. I placed my shaking butt on the varnished dresser making the glass vase shake as though it were walking, until it tipped over.

A large fat log of a pinky turned the handle of the window and flicked it open. The fingers were so big they left prints that looked like a bird's eye view of a rice terrace.

Are you the voice on the radio?

I'd been expecting this confrontation but it still frightened me. I had written a radio play about a creature confronting me over my radio voice, and therefore expected this meeting. The janitor said that I had predicted the future. This lessened the fear, but I couldn't shake it entirely.

It would have put the entire conversation at too weird an angle if I had looked out the window. The tree spirit was smoking a cigar and its glowing embers were lighting up the night. The smoke rings made clouds. I prayed that this orange red moon disc would alert the municipal authorities to the fact that I was being threatened by a kapre and that they could deploy lights and other modern technology to confuse him. *Where there is smoke, there is fire!*

There are endless accounts of encounters with this creature. He seems to be as common as tokoloshes are to Zulus. I don't know if there is only one giant who inhabits all the trees, or if there is a whole tribe of them, but I have heard stories from too many people I trust to doubt the existence of the kapre. Even if the kapre hadn't existed before people started talking about him, widespread belief in this creature would have conjured him up out of thin air long ago.

The kapre confronting me is an Elvis taxon from the north. They re-emerged when colonialists introduced a tobacco monoculture in the region, and the giants were seen to smoke cigars. Who rolled them such big cigars? What is their adoption rate for cigarettes?

I wasn't copying you, I said, though my mouth didn't appear to move. I knew he heard.

He leaned his back against the wall of the building, which shook, and stretched his legs, kicking away the painted mural of the beach. My buttocks stopped shaking. He was flicking blades of grass, or perhaps these were young tree saplings.

You're lying. His voice made the palms shake. The electric fan in my room started to speed up as if it were panicking, left, right, left, right, left, right, left, right.

I took ten deep breaths and I was still petrified.

And then I heard operatic singing that made my cheeks buzz like a tuning fork. At first I thought it was night creatures mating but it was a song, *Paloma, koo-koo-roo-koo-koo, Paloma. Koo-koo-roo-koo-koo* became *hu-hu-ru-hu-hu*. And then the crying *hu-hu-hu* became mocking, fiercer. *Hu hu hu*. I'd heard stories like this before, and I knew what to expect when I looked out the window. My bravery came from convincing myself that I had just invented everything. My imagination had eloped with local mythology. I knew there would be an old lady with the face of a dog outside my room. I looked out the window where the chickens were and I saw a little girl. She was curled up and when she stirred and turned her face towards me, it was the face of the pig.

Clog, clog, clog.

Leave us alone, the pig snorted, walking up to the window, raising her front hoofs up.

A talking horse came close, yelling, *tigidig, tigidig, tigidig*, mimicking the sound of its trotting because it was so quiet. *You're afraid of us. Afraid of making us real*, the horse said. *Tigidig, tigidig!*

Yeah, clog, clog, clog. And we are telling you, if you keep putting us on the radio, you will regret it.

Announcer: There was once a one-eyed kapre called Agyo, who fought against the Spanish when they came here in the fifteen hundreds. He had lived in relative peace, letting the datus settle their disputes without outside interference. But his cousin down in the Visayas had stood up once to give his own tree some *luften, luften*, and saw a group of men trying to cross the shore in leather vestments. Their awkward manner made him extremely suspicious. They were not from here, were they lost? The kapre pulled on the cord that tied all kapres together, an alarm network that the otherwise territorial creatures never used. After all, the world was still of a vague geography. They learnt from the energies in the South Americas what these conquistadors were about. Even if they could not quite understand it yet, they sensed immediately that once Christianity was imposed upon the local people they would still remain in the trees. They would blend in with the local fauna, they'd be mentioned in schoolyard stories, but they'd be feared.

I ran out of the condotel and cried for help, and for hours it seemed nobody could hear me except for a man who looked

familiar because he resembled a bloated version of a toothless
actor who'd starred in toothpaste ads when I was a child.
He was wearing combat fatigues, a beige vest and boots with
laces tied up in quadruple knots. The stink of his shoes was
trapped there until kingdom come.

The sun was about to rise but the air wasn't calm and balmy
like it usually was when Ma used to get up and send Saucisson
out for tikling. It was extremely hot.

I wasn't sure if my saviour understood the words
I'd cried out – *Help, please god help me!* and similar
variations. I don't like the word 'cry,' it sounds so sharp
and feels like getting my fingers stuck on an ice cube
from the freezer.

And then he came up to me, and examined me. He looked
like Jesus. I remembered seeing him in the market with his
open lips, picking up discarded cow skin and using it as a
coat. In that weather! He tucked his lips into his teeth as if
to say, *Feed me, throw a piece of bread into my hole-in-one.*
At the market, everyone ignored him but, at that point,
I needed his attention.

Can you help me? He mouthed the words back without
a sound. Some people are in the habit of repeating words
back to you, like an English teacher I once had who did
so as I read from a textbook about types of body language,
and I couldn't go on because I could see her mouth following
every word I spoke.

He opened his mouth then he looked up, forgetting his
previous role as echo chamber. He said, *The volcano is
going to…*

What?

I turned around and saw a bright red glow, which at first
I mistook for the end of a cigar. There were people running
out of their homes with open suitcases in their hands, the
tricycles, the jeeps, the Butterfly bus, the bar flies, the kids
with Supersonics jerseys, the decomposing body of Jerry,
Yeung Bi Bi, Ma…

Clear out! Clear out, everybody! The volcano is – !
The volcano is – !

The volcano is…!

Aliasing
Mara Coson
Semina No. 9
Published and distributed by Book Works, London

© Mara Coson, 2018

ISBN 978 1 906012 80 9

Commissioning editor: Stewart Home
Edited by Stewart Home and Gavin Everall
Proofread by Rebecca Bligh
Designed by Fraser Muggeridge studio
Printed by Tallinn Book Printers

Book Works
19 Holywell Row
London
EC2A 4JB
www.bookworks.org.uk
tel: +44 (0)20 7247 2203

Book Works is funded by Arts Council England

Supported using public funding by
**ARTS COUNCIL
ENGLAND**